FREAK SHOW

**Other Apple Paperbacks
by Jahnna N. Malcolm**

The Slime That Ate Crestview

Scared to Death

Scared Stiff

FREAK SHOW

Jahnna N. Malcolm

AN
APPLE
PAPERBACK

SCHOLASTIC INC.
New York Toronto London Auckland Sydney

ISBN 0-590-45853-1

12 11 10 9 8 7 6 5 4 3 2   4 5 6 7 8/9

Printed in the U.S.A.   40

First Scholastic printing, March 1993

*For Jill and Andrew Dunlap
(share this with Tom and Julia)*

FREAK SHOW

Chapter One

His eyes were watching her. Katie was certain of it. The wizard's dark brows arched evilly over his long hooked nose as he stared out from the painted front of the carnival funhouse. GREYWOLD'S PHANTASMAGORIA, read the ornate lettering above the picture. At one time it must have shimmered with brilliant color, but now the paint was faded and peeling.

"You guys, this place gives me the creeps," Katie Rolfing whispered. "I don't think we should go in there."

"It'll be fun!" Quinn Feldman said. The twelve-year-old dug in the pocket of her jean skirt for her two remaining carnival tickets. "Now come on."

Katie shook her blonde hair. "That building's a wreck."

"That's probably why they hid it behind the public restrooms," Skip Callahan said, sticking his broad, freckled face between the two girls. "So parents wouldn't see it and get upset."

"This funhouse looks old because it is," Trevor Jackson said. "See?" The black seventh-grader, who towered over the other three, pointed to the upper right-hand corner of the sign. "Estab-lished in 1906."

"Wow!" Skip exclaimed. "That means it's nearly a hundred years old."

"That settles it," Katie said, folding her arms firmly across her chest. "I'm never going in that place."

Quinn flipped her wavy brown hair over one shoulder. "I swear, Katie, you are such a scaredy-cat."

"I am not," Katie protested.

"Are too," Skip Callahan said, imitating her voice perfectly. "You didn't want to go on the Octopus, you said the Scrambler was too scary, and you chickened out of the Bullet ride, too."

Trevor put one hand on Katie's shoulder and shook his head in mock sadness. "I hate to say it, Katie, but you win the Chicken Little Wimp of the World award." He held out his other hand to Skip. "Skipper, the award, please."

Skip, who had managed to win four stuffed bears, a pair of pink fuzzy dice, and a rubber chicken at the darts game on the midway, flopped the rubber chicken onto Trevor's open hand. "Here it is. Let her have it."

Katie grabbed the rubber chicken and batted it against Skip's shoulder. "I'll show you who's a chicken. Take that. And that. And that!"

"Yeow!" Skip stumbled backward into the side of the funhouse and a large wooden board crashed to the ground, landing on his foot. "Ooh, that smarts!" He clutched his left foot in his hand and hopped around in a circle. "Yeowee."

"Serves you right," Quinn said primly.

Trevor bent down to pick up the board. "Hey, you guys," he whispered. "Take a look at this."

Katie and Quinn huddled with Trevor and Skip around the weathered panel of wood. Instead of the magician's face, pictures of strange characters from a carnival sideshow had been painted upon it.

"What about it?" Quinn said. "It's just an old sign."

"Not quite." Trevor pointed to some words scrawled across the board in shaky handwriting. "Look at the message."

"What does it say?" Katie asked.

Trevor cocked his head to the side and read the words out loud. *"Abandon all hope, ye who enter here."*

Suddenly a cold breeze whipped its way through

3

the carnival, pulling paper cones topped with pink cotton candy out of children's hands, and launching several purple-and-green balloons high into the sky. It went through Katie's light jacket, sending a shiver that felt like ice water up her spine.

The gust of wind was so strong that it ripped the sign right out of Trevor's hands. Then a cloud of thick dust swirled up around them, covering the lenses of Trevor's glasses in a thin layer of light brown dirt. "I'm blind!" he yelped.

"My hair!" Quinn spun in a circle to avoid the dust.

"Yeow!" Skip yelled, rubbing his eyes with his knuckles. "I've got something in my eye."

While her friends choked and waved their hands at the dust, Katie glanced nervously up at the sky. Ominous black clouds swirled overhead, reminding her of another one of her pet fears — tornadoes. Before Katie could think anymore about it, she glanced at the painted sign above the funhouse and caught her breath. The hideous face of Greywold the Magician was now staring directly down at her!

"His face!" she gasped. "It's moved."

"What?" Quinn mumbled.

Katie pointed a trembling finger up at the eerie sign. "The — the magician. A minute ago he was in profile. Now he's staring right at us."

Trevor, who was wiping the dust off his glasses with his shirt, looked up and scoffed. "Katie, you're the jumpiest person I know."

"No kidding," Skip agreed with a teasing grin. "I bet you check under the bed and in the closet before you go to sleep at night."

Katie shrugged. She wasn't about to admit it, but not only did she check under the bed and in the closet, she also slept with the covers pulled up to her chin and a very strong night-light shining over her dresser.

"Good evening!" a voice rasped from behind them. "We've been waiting for you."

All four children nearly jumped out of their skins. Katie turned to run and bumped directly into the chest of a huge, bald man. Rolls of skin drooped over his eyes and furrowed the back of his neck. The muscular arms bulging out of his striped T-shirt were covered in tattoos. Strange tattoos. Flying dragons and bug-eyed gargoyles, with words written in a language Katie had never seen before.

"Are ye coming into the fun house, or not?" he asked in a strange accent that made him sound like a pirate. "We don't much care for loiterers."

"We are going in, sir," Quinn answered in her politest voice. "We were just making sure we had the correct number of tickets." Then she flashed the man her pert smile — the one that usually charmed most adults — and added, "Does this one cost two?"

"You know it." The man with the gleaming dome of a head stared at Quinn for so long that her smile melted completely off her face.

"There." Trevor thrust eight tickets into the big man's hand. "That's for all of us." Then Trevor turned to Katie, Skip, and Quinn. "Come on. We've paid. Now let's go in."

Katie knew it was silly to be afraid, but there was something about this funhouse and the man taking the tickets that just didn't *feel* right.

"You guys go in without me," she cried, backing away from the rickety structure. "I'll wait for you over by the bathrooms."

Quinn shook her head in exasperation. "Katie, I really wish you'd come with us. It'll be fun!"

"Maybe another time," Katie called feebly from the bench just outside the public rest rooms.

Skip shrugged. "Okay, Katie. See you soon." He stepped up to the tattooed man and asked, "Where do we go?"

The man's harsh mouth transformed into a smile and he said, "You follow me. Through this door and into a world like none you've ever seen before."

Katie watched her friends disappear through

6

the archway into the darkened interior of the funhouse, and tried hard to ignore the queasy feeling in her stomach. She hadn't noticed before, but the entrance itself was very unusual. On each side of the wooden archway crouched a leering gargoyle carved out of wood and painted in garish colors.

She didn't dare raise her eyes to look at the sign above the entrance for fear she might meet the magician's eyes again. Instead, Katie focused all of her energy on hoping her friends would be all right.

"Of course they'll be okay," she told herself. "You're just being silly."

Trevor, Skip, and Quinn were three of the most popular kids at Woodrow Wilson Middle School. Good things always happened to them.

Sometimes Katie wondered why they included her in their tightly knit group. Most of the time she was fun to be around. But occasionally her fears got in the way of having a good time. She was afraid of the dark. And thunder. And heights. Which eliminated hide-and-go-seek at night, playing outside during rainstorms, and climbing trees.

"Katie!"

She turned around to see one of her classmates calling from a concession wagon along the midway. "What are you doing back here?" Elizabeth Thomson asked.

Katie didn't want to confess that she was afraid of the funhouse, so she crossed her fingers behind her back and said, "I'm just resting. These rides have really worn me out."

"You're kidding." Elizabeth, clutching a snow cone in one hand and two stuffed pandas in the other, joined Katie on the bench. "This carnival is so dinky, I think I've played every game on the midway and ridden all of the rides twice."

"Well, what did you expect to come to Wheaton, Nebraska?" Katie asked. "The Barnum and Bailey circus?"

Elizabeth sighed heavily, "Of course not. It's just that I expected something a little . . . a little more wild."

"Gee," Katie said. "I thought the Bullet looked pretty wild. Trevor, Skip, and Quinn screamed their brains out the entire time they were on it."

"Where are those guys, anyway?" Elizabeth asked as she took a big bite of her snow cone.

"In the funhouse," Katie replied.

"What funhouse?" Elizabeth mumbled through a mouthful of chipped ice. A thin stream of red juice ran out of the side of her mouth and she hurriedly dabbed at it with her hand. "I didn't see a funhouse, and I've covered every inch of this silly carnival."

Katie stared at Elizabeth for what seemed like a full minute. How could she be so dense? "Phantasmagoria," Katie said. "It's right over there."

She gestured with her thumb to the building behind them as a deafening clap of thunder exploded above their heads. A blinding flash of light zigzagged across the sky and struck the funhouse, showering sparks everywhere.

Every light for miles blinked out and for one brief moment everything was silent. Then hundreds of terrified screams shattered the air.

Chapter Two

Katie felt like she couldn't breathe. She'd always been afraid of the dark and now the night had turned so black she couldn't see her hand in front of her face.

The hoarse cries of parents calling for their children mingled with the terrified screams of kids trapped on the rides.

"Hey, you boys," a barker on the carnival midway shouted. "Stay away from those prizes!"

Elizabeth had run off the instant the lightning struck the funhouse, but Katie stayed glued to the wooden bench. She would have remained there if some boys running down the aisles, whooping at the top of their lungs, hadn't crashed into her.

The bench lurched forward and the next thing Katie knew she was face down in the dirt. The jolt brought her to her senses and she remembered her friends who were still trapped inside that awful funhouse.

"Quinn?" Katie called into the blackness as she pulled herself to her feet. "Trevor? Skip?"

Katie groped at the air in front of her and walked stiff-legged toward where she thought the funhouse should be. If Quinn and the boys were still inside, they were probably trying to feel their way to the exit. Maybe her voice would guide them.

"You guys! It's Katie!" she shouted, inching her way forward.

Off in the distance, the calliope on the merry-go-round wheezed "Three Blind Mice" at an eerily slow speed. Then it sped up to normal as the carnival's backup generator revved to life. One by one the outline of each ride became visible against the night sky and the screams faded away. Katie kept walking forward, knowing that any second the lights would come back on in her corner of the fairgrounds.

Suddenly her fingertips brushed the surface of something rough and flat. It felt like weathered canvas. Katie didn't remember any awnings or side flaps hanging from the funhouse but she pushed on it anyway. Instantly her nostrils were filled with the heavy aroma of burning incense.

"Hello there, little girl," an old voice cracked. "Come to visit Annie Entwhistle, have you?"

Katie sprang back in alarm. As her eyes adjusted to the dim light, she saw that she had stum-

11

bled into a small tent. A single candle burned on a card table in its center.

"Wh — where am I?" Katie stammered.

A tiny old woman with stringy gray hair leaned forward into the candle's glow. Hundreds of wrinkles caused by too many years in the harsh sun creased her leathery skin. A wooden matchstick dangled from the corner of her mouth. "Where do you wish to be?" the old lady asked.

What Katie wanted to say was, *Home. Safe in my bed and away from all of this*, but the words that came out of her mouth were, "I'm looking for my friends. They were in the funhouse. I thought it was right here but I — I must have gotten turned around."

"Everything is turned around." The woman narrowed her cloudy blue eyes to two little slits. "It happened — like that!" She snapped her fingers and the candle flared.

At the same moment the tent flap opened and an immense bald head loomed in the gap. It was the tattooed man who'd taken her friends' tickets. Katie pressed herself into the dark corner of the tent, hoping he wouldn't see her.

"Somethin's wrong, Annie. Lightning struck and everything went haywire," the bald man muttered, shaking his head. "The master's not going to like it at all, at all."

Annie took the matchstick out of her mouth and pursed her lips. Little hairs bristled out around

12

them. "I knew it," she mumbled, half to herself. "My nose was twitching, and my toes were a-tingling."

The bald man stepped into the tent. "What should we do?"

The old lady jerked her head back suddenly. Her eyes rolled up into their sockets until only the whites showed. Katie bit her hand and tried not to cry out.

Annie Entwhistle rocked back and forth gently, mumbling a few words over and over again that Katie couldn't understand. Finally the old woman heaved a large sigh and opened her eyes. "I don't know. My pictures are hazy, I can't make 'em out."

The bald man slammed his tattooed palm on the table. "What good's a fortune teller if you can't tell me anything?" he snapped. The candle flickered and sputtered and almost went out.

"Fortune teller!" Katie gasped out loud. She had always thought fortune tellers wore long, colorful print skirts and jeweled turbans. Annie Entwhistle was wearing drab overalls and a faded plaid shirt with a patch clumsily sewn over one elbow.

At the sound of Katie's voice, the huge man spun and faced her. "What are ye doin' here?" he growled as Katie cowered in the corner. "Only carnies are allowed in the living quarters."

"You *live* here?" Katie asked the old lady.

"That depends on what you mean by live," Annie Entwhistle replied dryly. "This is where I spend my days, year in and year out, watching — "

"That's enough!" the thug shouted. Then he flipped open the tent flap and barked at Katie, "Out with you. And I'd better not see your face around here again."

Katie ducked under his tattooed arm and scurried outside. Loud tinny music and the smell of buttered popcorn once again filled the air. People were laughing and talking, and for a moment it was almost as if nothing had happened. Almost.

Katie glanced nervously over her shoulder at Annie Entwhistle's tent. The light from the single candle glowed dimly through the drab canvas. Her little tent looked like a relic from another time, hemmed in by campers, trailers, and RV's.

Directly across from Annie's tent was the funhouse. The lightning hadn't damaged the building, but it was the only carnival attraction whose lights hadn't been turned back on. It looked completely deserted.

"Skip, Quinn, and Trevor must have come out already," Katie said looking over her shoulder. But before she could make a step toward the midway, a movement at the funhouse exit caught her eye. It was Skip. He raced down the ramp and right past Katie. His eyes were two huge circles in his face and he ran as if something terrible were chasing him. Skip didn't stop running until he

14

reached the concession stand on the edge of the midway.

"Please, please," he rasped. "Give me the biggest Coke you have."

Quinn stumbled down the ramp next. Her eyes were glazed and she spun in a circle, murmuring, "Wait for me. I'm lost."

Katie hurried to Quinn. She grabbed her by the shoulders and shook her gently. Quinn's whole body was limp and her arms flopped like spaghetti at her sides.

"Quinn?" Katie asked, trying to get her to focus on her face. "Quinn, it's me, Katie. Are you okay?"

"Katie?" Quinn tilted her chin skyward and blinked her big blue eyes. "Where am I?"

"You're at the carnival. You just went into the Phantasmagoria Funhouse."

"I did?" Quinn's jaw hung slackly and her words were slurred. "I don't remember."

Katie shot a glance back over her shoulder at Skip. His hands were shaking so violently that he could barely pay for his drink.

"This is really scary," Katie said out loud. "I don't like this at all."

"Where's Trevor?" Quinn asked numbly.

"That's what I was going to ask you," Katie said, still holding Quinn tightly by the shoulders. "The three of you paid your tickets and went into the funhouse. I watched you."

Quinn licked her lips. "I'm thirsty. Really thirsty."

"Quinn, please," Katie urged. "What's going on?"

"Trevor!" Quinn interrupted, pointing at the funhouse exit.

Katie watched in horror as Trevor crawled down the funhouse ramp on his hands and knees. When he reached the bottom, his shoulders heaved and he threw up.

By nature Katie was a follower, not a leader. But she knew that she had to take charge now. Gently but firmly she ushered Quinn to the overturned bench by the rest rooms, set it upright with one hand and then very carefully made her friend sit down.

"Wait here," she ordered.

Skip was still standing by the concession stand, clutching his Coke and looking very disoriented.

"Skip," Katie called. "Skip Callahan. Come here and sit down."

Skip, who usually had a wisecrack for everyone, just nodded. He shuffled across the dusty aisle and took a seat on the bench beside Quinn, who was staring blankly at her hands in her lap.

Katie hurried over to Trevor. He had pulled himself to his feet and was leaning against the railing of the exit ramp. "We have to go," he choked. "Now."

16

"Trevor, what happened in there?" Katie whispered.

He put one hand to his forehead and squeezed his eyes shut. "I — I'm not sure. One second we were going through this maze. I think someone pushed us into a room full of mirrors and — and then . . ." Trevor stared off blankly into space.

"And then?" Katie urged.

"Something happened."

"What kind of something?"

Trevor shook his head. "I'm not sure. But everything went black and I felt like my whole body had been put in a blender."

"I knew you guys shouldn't have gone inside the funhouse." Katie looped her arm through his and helped Trevor to the bench where Quinn and Skip were still sitting. "The same thing must have happened to them. Look at Skip. His hands are shaking."

At the sound of his name, Skip stood up shakily. He saw Trevor and blurted, "We have to go home."

"He's right," Quinn chimed in. "We have to leave."

Trevor nodded. "And leave *now*."

Katie eyed her friends warily. Something seemed different about them. They'd all had a very bad scare, but there was something else. Something she couldn't quite put her finger on.

"We'll get you guys home," Katie said cheerily. "Then you can get a good night's sleep and forget about this hick carnival and stupid old funhouse. Tomorrow it will all just seem like a bad dream."

Katie wished she felt as sure as she sounded. The truth was, she was dreading going to sleep that night. Katie had a feeling that grotesque images of the strange fortune teller and the bald man with the hideous tattoos would probably haunt her dreams and keep her awake all night.

She was right.

Chapter Three

"**E**arth to Katie. Helloooooh. Anybody home?"

A hand waved back and forth in front of Katie Rolfing's half-closed eyes. It belonged to her science teacher, Mr. Welder.

Katie snapped to attention. Science wasn't her best subject and it was never a good idea to get caught napping in Mr. Welder's class. "I'm here, I'm here," she babbled. "I was just trying to think of the answer."

"To what question?" Mr. Welder asked with a smirk.

"The one on the board."

A wave of giggles rippled around the classroom and Katie looked sideways at the green chalkboard. Just her luck — it was blank. Katie flashed the redheaded teacher a sheepish grin. "Oops."

"*Oops* is what Miss Rolfing says we get when we combine hydrogen and oxygen," the teacher said sarcastically. "Most people would say you get water and a pretty loud explosion but Miss Rolfing tells us it's *oops*."

This time the whole class burst out laughing.

Katie could feel her cheeks heat up. Mr. Welder never missed an opportunity to humiliate one of his students. She wished Quinn were there. Quinn would have crossed her eyes and stuck out her tongue behind Mr. Welder's back. That would have made Katie feel better. But Quinn wasn't there. Her desk right across the aisle was empty.

That's what had distracted Katie from the morning's lesson. It was so unlike Quinn to miss school. Katie couldn't help thinking that it had something to do with their bizarre experience at the carnival the night before.

"If *oops* is what we get when we combine hydrogen and oxygen," Mr. Welder continued, "what do we get when we combine hydrogen, oxygen, and sulfur? *Yeowie?*"

Before Katie could say *sulfuric acid,* a deep bong rang from the PA speaker above the door at the back of the class.

"Class dismissed," Mr. Welder shouted over the babble of voices and clatter of desks opening and shutting.

Katie leapt straight out of her seat and bolted for the door, partly because she didn't want to spend another minute with Mr. Welder, but mostly because she needed to find Trevor or Skip. And she only had ten minutes to do it.

Woodrow Wilson Middle School was an old three-story brick building. All of the lockers were on the main floor, along with the cafeteria. Katie took the marble stairs two at a time and nearly crashed right into Trevor.

"I don't believe it," he was muttering to himself. "I just don't believe it."

"Trevor?" Katie asked anxiously. "Has something happened to Quinn?"

He shook his head. "No, me. I flunked my math test."

Katie blinked several times. Trevor never flunked *anything*. "What happened?"

"I'm not sure," he replied. "Mrs. Thomas passed out the tests like usual. But when I looked down, I suddenly started itching all over, like I had fleas, or something. Then I — *woof*!"

"What did you say?"

"Woof! Woof!" Trevor clapped his hand over his mouth and his eyes bugged out in shock.

"Do you have a temperature?" Katie reached up and felt his forehead. "Maybe you're sick."

"I feel fine." Trevor batted at his ear with one hand, like a dog scratching a flea. He stopped and whispered, "Or at least I *thought* I felt fine."

Katie grabbed him by the elbow and guided him to the tiny alcove under the stairs. She had to talk to him in private and the crowded hall was anything but that.

"Trevor," she whispered, "do you think what's

21

happening to you has anything to do with last night?"

"What happened last night?" he asked.

"You don't re — ?" Katie started to shout, then quickly caught herself and repeated in a hushed voice, "You really don't remember?"

"What's there to remember?" Suddenly Trevor raised his nose and sniffed the air intently. Then he turned back to Katie as if nothing had happened. "We went to the carnival, rode a few rides, ate some pretty horrible food, and came home."

Katie put her hands on her hips. "You mean to tell me you don't remember throwing up?"

Trevor shrugged. "Like I said, the food was pretty bad."

Suddenly he was seized by another scratching fit, this time under his arm. As Trevor clawed at his armpit, his foot thumped loudly on the wooden floor.

Katie narrowed her eyes at him. Trevor was acting very strangely. She couldn't tell if he was just kidding around, or if he'd caught a bad case of poison ivy. But before Katie could press him further, a very loud, familiar voice bellowed, "Let go of me, lizard lips!"

Skip Callahan was being marched down the center of the crowded hall by a muscular boy with a crew cut and a thick neck. It was Fritz Lazarde, the ninth-grade hall monitor. He had Skip by the collar of his rugby shirt.

"Looks like Skip's in trouble. I wonder what happened?" Katie gasped to Trevor.

"I don't know but he must have done something terrible 'cause Lazarde is taking him to the vice principal's office."

"Skip never does anything terrible," Katie mumbled. "He's the nicest guy in school."

"Aw, come on, Fritz. I'm innocent," Skip said, twisting around to face the other boy. "You know it and I know it."

He gave Fritz a friendly pat on the back. To everyone's amazement, Fritz flew four feet across the hall and slammed into a bank of lockers. He clutched his head, and glared at Skip.

"That's it for you, Callahan," Fritz muttered between clenched teeth. "Once Mr. Quintero hears about this, you'll be suspended for life."

Trevor, who was standing next to Katie, curled his lip in a snarl and let out a low threatening growl. For half a second Katie thought she was standing next to her dog, Britty.

"Now, Trevor," Katie warned, "don't you get in trouble, too. Fighting is mandatory suspension."

Trevor blinked several times and then cleared his throat. "Fritz?" he asked. "What's going on?"

Fritz Lazarde was still holding his head as he straightened up. "I caught Skip destroying school property."

"That's a lie," Skip retorted.

"Oh, yeah?" Fritz held up the remains of a metal locker door. "Then tell me how this happened?"

Skip looked at the twisted metal and shrugged. "I'm not sure. I remember turning the combination on my lock and unhooking the latch. Then suddenly the door was off its hinges."

"Yeah, right." Fritz looked at Skip in disgust. "I've got fifty witnesses who saw you rip this door off and heave it across the hall."

"It slipped out of my hands," Skip cut in.

"Then you went in the boys' room and slammed the bathroom door against the wall so hard that the handle dug a crater in the plaster."

"What?" Skip gasped. "I don't remember that."

"Kenny Marshall said you squeezed his hand so hard he heard his bones crunch."

"I was just being friendly."

"Some friend," Fritz growled. "Kenny's with the school nurse right this minute. She's checking for broken bones."

Katie looked down at Skip's hands. They did look a lot brawnier than she remembered. She looked up at Skip's confused face. "Gee, Skip, it sounds like you don't know your own strength."

"What strength?" Skip muttered. "I can barely do three push-ups in gym class. There's no way that I could crush Kenny's hand."

"Right." Fritz threw open the door to the vice principal's office and called to the secretary, "I need to see Mr. Quintero."

Skip squeezed his eyes shut and shook his head. "I just don't get it. This morning I went to brush my teeth and snapped my toothbrush in half. Then I kicked a soccer ball in gym and it burst. And now this . . ." He put his hands to his head. "Something weird is happening to me, and I don't know what it is."

"Tell it to Mr. Quintero," Fritz snapped as he pulled Skip into the vice principal's office.

The door swung shut and Trevor called, "Hang in there, Skip!"

"See you after school," Katie added, feebly. "The usual place."

Trevor and Katie stared at the closed door for a few seconds. The hall was emptying quickly as the students hurried to their next class. Suddenly Trevor snapped his fingers.

"The moon!" he exclaimed. "That's it! It's got to be the moon."

"The moon?" Katie squinted one eye shut and stared at Trevor. "What are you talking about?"

"They say the full moon can make people say and do strange things." Trevor flashed her a big smile. "That would explain why I cratered my math test and have this urge to howl. And why Skipper has turned into the Incredible Hulk."

"I wish it were so simple," Katie said. "But whatever it is, I have a feeling Quinn is going through the same thing as you and Skip. She's not in school today — "

"I'm here, I'm here," a voice mumbled from behind them.

"Quinn!" Katie felt a wave of relief sweep over her. "I was really worried about you. I thought something terrible might have happened."

"It did," Quinn grumbled, rubbing her eyes with the heels of her hands and yawning. "I overslept."

Katie couldn't believe how awful Quinn looked. She had actually come to school with her hair uncombed. Usually Quinn spent a least a half an hour on her face alone, putting just a touch of mascara on her lashes, blusher on her cheeks, and Barely There gloss on her lips, but today she wore no makeup at all. Quinn's face even had a bloated look to it.

"Didn't your mom wake you?" Katie asked.

Quinn shook her head. "She forgot. And then when I did get up it took me an hour to eat breakfast."

"An hour?" Trevor repeated. "What did you eat?"

"Four eggs, six slices of bacon, two pieces of toast, a slice of melon, a bowl of Cheerios, and . . ." She paused, squinting one eye shut in thought. "A couple of waffles."

"You ate all of that?" Katie gasped. "No way!"

"Even I couldn't eat that much," Trevor murmured. "You must feel terrible."

"No." Quinn shook her tangled mass of hair.

"Hungry. I'm starved. What's on the menu today?"

"Mystery meat loaf, vegetable medley, and banana mash," Trevor rattled off without hesitation.

"Oh, gross," Katie said, wrinkling her nose. "No wonder so many kids brought their lunch."

"It sounds delicious," Quinn said seriously.

"You must be sick," Katie declared. "In all of the years we've gone to school together, you've never touched that meat loaf."

BRRRRRRRING!

All three of them jumped at the sound. The final bell seemed louder than usual in the deserted hallway.

"Yikes!" Katie shouted. "We're late."

"Oh, great," Trevor groaned as he ran for the stairs. "Mr. Meyers hates tardiness more than anything. He'll probably dock me a whole grade."

Katie hurried after Trevor. At the landing Katie looked behind her and saw that Quinn hadn't moved. "Come on, Quinn!"

Quinn looked up at her and shrugged. "I've already missed half the day. What's one more class? Besides, I'm a little hungry. Maybe I'll get a snack from the vending machine."

Quinn never cut class. Ever. But Katie didn't have time to discuss it. She raced for the third floor and tiptoed down the hall to Mrs. Thomas's Honors English on the far end of the building.

The rest of the class was already bent over their

desks copying Mrs. Thomas's notes from the board as Katie slipped into the room. She sat down at her desk as quietly as possible and flipped open her notebook. But instead of copying the notes on the board, Katie found herself making a list of what had happened to her friends.

Trevor flunked a math test and has started itching and barking like a dog.

Skip tore the door of his locker, knocked Fritz across the hall, bashed a hole in the bathroom wall, and crushed Kenny Marshall's hand.

Quinn overslept and came to school looking like a bloated slob. She ate a breakfast large enough for an army, then decided to cut class so she could get a snack.

Katie nibbled thoughtfully on her pencil as she tried to come up with an explanation for her friends' bizarre behavior. When the bolt of lightning knocked out the lights at the carnival, could something inside the funhouse have fallen on their heads, giving them a group concussion? She decided to urge all of them to see the school nurse when she talked to them after school.

However, when school ended, something happened that made Katie forget all about the school nurse.

The four of them met at their usual meeting spot by the bike racks. They walked home with the sun in their eyes. At the corner of Fourth and Oak the boys said good-bye and turned down Fourth Street in the direction of Skip's house. Katie raised her hand to wave and froze in her tracks.

Something was wrong with the boys' shadows. The hideous misshapen forms looming on the ground behind Skip and Trevor did not match their bodies at all.

Katie gasped and turned to tell Quinn to look when suddenly she caught a glimpse of Quinn's shadow. It, too, was strange — huge and round, and nothing at all like her friend.

In that instant, Katie realized that the monstrous shadows following her friends were not their own!

Chapter Four

"**Q**uinn!" Katie screamed. "Look behind you!"

Quinn covered her head with her arms, as if she thought she were about to be hit. "What? Where? I don't see anything."

"The shadow. On — on the ground," Katie stammered. "It — it's not yours."

"Get serious."

Katie placed her right hand across her heart and declared, "As your best friend, I'm telling you I have never been so serious in my entire life." She clenched her teeth and hissed, "Now *look behind you.*"

Quinn sighed and, turning her head slowly, peered over her shoulder. She had stepped under a big elm tree and the broad leafy outline of the tree covered the sidewalk. "Katie, that's just the tree."

"No, Quinn," Katie persisted. "Step back into the light. You'll see."

"No way." Quinn folded her arms stubbornly. "This is silly. What's gotten into you, anyway?"

"Me? You're the one who was late for school and didn't comb her hair. That's not like you at all — "

"I'm hungry," Quinn cut in abruptly. "I could eat an entire jumbo size pizza with the works all by myself."

As Quinn spoke, her eyes seemed to glaze over and get smaller. And her face appeared to be getting puffier by the second.

"Or how about fudge?" Quinn smacked her lips. "An entire pan of frosted fudge brownies."

Katie stared at her friend in amazement. "But you never eat chocolate."

Quinn puffed out her lower lip in a pout, which made her face look even chubbier. "I'd eat chocolate if you gave me some."

"Well, we probably have some Oreos at my house — "

"Oreos!" Quinn clapped her hands together with glee. "Little chocolate and vanilla sandwiches. They're the best."

"If we don't have Oreos," Katie said as she led Quinn through the mottled shadows of the tree-lined street, "there's always ice cream."

"Oh, goody!" Quinn squealed.

Katie turned away. She didn't want Quinn to see the confused look on her face. Quinn Feldman *never* ate fattening foods like chocolate, ice cream, or cookies, and she would *never* in a million years say something as nerdy as, "Oh, goody!" unless she was being very sarcastic.

When they stepped through Katie's front door, Quinn pushed ahead of Katie and made a beeline for the kitchen. It was hard for Katie to believe but Quinn was starting to waddle as she walked.

Thunk!

The kitchen cupboards were flung open. Katie heard the sound of plastic wrappers being ripped apart, followed by a gross collection of slurps and grunts.

"Quinn?" she called tentatively toward the kitchen. "Are you all right?"

"*Snort*," came the muffled answer. "Ummmm. Good!"

"She's not only eating like a pig," Katie grumbled under her breath, "she's beginning to sound like one, too." Katie headed down the hall to her bedroom calling, "Look, Quinn, I'm going to put my books away. I'll be back in a minute."

"Ice cream! *Wheeeee!*" was Quinn's reply.

Katie tossed her books on her bed and hurried over to the telephone on her bedside table. She had to call Skip and Trevor right away. Something very strange was happening to Quinn and they should know about it. She dialed Skip's number first and waited. The phone rang ten times before someone answered. Katie heard a loud crash, followed by an "Ow!" Finally a voice said, "Callahan residence."

"Mr. Callahan?" Katie asked. "May I talk to Skip, please?"

"Speaking," the deep voice replied.

"Skip?" Katie could hardly believe her ears. His voice seemed to have dropped two octaves. "Do you have a cold?"

"No," the voice mumbled. "Why?"

"You — you just sound so. . . so *different*. Is something wrong?"

"I'm not sure," Skip replied. "I seemed to have turned into the biggest klutz on earth. I bump into furniture, trip over things, and just now I took a swig of my Coke and completely crushed the can."

"Wow," Katie murmured.

"And here's the really weird part — I think I'm having a growth spurt."

"A growth spurt?" Katie repeated.

"Yeah, Mom says it happens to guys my age. I just didn't think it happened in one day."

"Gee, Skip," Katie said. "I don't think it does."

"*Whooaa!* Here it comes again!" Skip bellowed. "Sorry, Katie, gotta run."

Crash!

The phone, or Skip, or both, seemed to have hit the ground. "Are you okay?" Katie called out but the line was dead.

She set the phone back on the hook and mumbled, "What is going on?" She glanced out her window at the house behind hers. That's where Trevor lived. Katie decided to go over and personally find out what he thought of the whole situation.

"Quinn," Katie called as she hurried down the hall. "I'm going over to Trevor's for a minute. Want to come?"

"Nope," came the muffled reply. "I'm still eating."

Katie wondered how long Quinn would be able to keep it up. She was pretty sure the refrigerator didn't have much left in it. Her parents always did their grocery shopping on Friday and the cupboard got pretty bare by the end of the week.

She stopped at the sliding glass door that opened onto her backyard. "I'll be right back," she shouted. "Don't make too much of a mess, okay? My folks will be home pretty soon."

Katie cut across her backyard to the hedge. There was a small opening at one corner that she and Trevor had created when they were in kindergarten. They'd used it so much to come and go between the two houses that it had worn into a natural archway. Katie crawled through it and stood up on the other side.

All of the shades and curtains were drawn at Trevor's house and his parents' car was gone but Katie could clearly hear loud barking coming from indoors. She also heard a series of crashes and rattles, as if someone were clearing out a closet by dumping the contents on the floor. She crossed to the sliding glass door on the Jacksons' patio and knocked hard.

"Trevor, it's me," Katie shouted. "Did you guys get a dog?"

She waited a full minute, then knocked again. There was still no answer so Katie moved to the kitchen window and banged on that. Then she circled the entire house, beating on each of the ground-floor windows as she went. Finally she stopped and stared up at Trevor's bedroom window.

"I know you're in there, Trevor," Katie yelled, "Because I can hear you crashing around. What's going on?"

Suddenly the curtain in his window flew back and a furry brown face with two pointy ears and a short stubby snout appeared.

"Aaaah!" Katie leapt back in shock, clutching her hands to her heart.

Two unblinking brown eyes stared down at her for just a moment. Then the curtain shut and the half-man, half-dog was gone.

Katie took several deep breaths trying to figure out what it was that she had just seen. The creature was way too tiny to be Trevor. It had to be —

"Winston?" Katie yelled at the window. "Winston, is that you?"

Winston was Trevor's seven-year-old brother. He was always dressing up in goofy disguises and trying to scare everyone in the neighborhood. This was certainly the most convincing one he'd ever used.

"If you're trying to scare me with that weird mask, it worked," Katie chuckled halfheartedly. "Now tell Trevor to come to the window. I have to talk to him."

The curtain didn't move.

"Come on, Winston," Katie pleaded. "It's important." She waited a few more seconds but nothing happened. "Okay, you little creep, I'm going home. You be sure to tell Trevor to call me."

With that Katie spun on her heel and marched back to the hedge. She dropped to her hands and knees and crawled back through the opening. "What day is this?" she muttered. "April first?"

Katie grinned as she stood up and brushed the dirt off the knees of her jeans and palms of her hands. "I get it now. It *is* the first of April. It's April Fools' Day! And everyone's playing jokes on me."

Still chuckling to herself, Katie slid open the glass doors to her home and nearly choked. Empty Tupperware containers and used-up cartons of ice cream lay strewn all over the rug in the den.

"Quinn!" Katie raced into the kitchen. "Stop that this minute. What do you think you're doing?"

Quinn was behind the door of the refrigerator,

peering inside. She straightened up and took a very long swallow of milk right out of the carton.

"That's disgusting," Katie exclaimed. "Now put that down."

Quinn lowered the carton, closed the refrigerator door, and turned to look at her.

Katie's mouth dropped open in shock. Standing in front of her was a fat girl with flabby arms, a huge belly and, most incredible of all, a *beard*.

"Who are you?" Katie demanded, backing away in a panic toward the door. "And what are you doing in my refrigerator?"

The fat girl cocked her head in confusion. "I'm Quinn. And I'm eating."

"Quinn?" Katie's eyes nearly bugged out of her head. "Are you sure it's you?"

Quinn dropped her arms to her side. "Well, of course it's me. What kind of a stupid question is that?"

Katie's knees went weak. A bearded fat girl who sounded just like Quinn was eating everything in her kitchen. But how could it be Quinn? It just wasn't possible.

"What have you done with my friend?" Katie demanded. "And why are you wrecking her clothes?" She gestured to the denim skirt the bearded girl was wearing. It was torn at the seams. And the purple top looked like it was about to explode.

"Katie, get a grip."

37

There was no mistaking that voice. It had to be Quinn.

"It *is* you." Katie inched closer to her friend. "But what's happened?"

"I have no idea what you're talking about," Quinn replied.

Katie grabbed Quinn by the pudgy hand and pulled her into the living room. A large mirror hung above the fireplace and Katie shoved the girl in front of it. "There," she said. "Take a good look at yourself."

Quinn sighed impatiently and did as she was told.

Two figures stood reflected in the mirror. One was a tall, thin girl with limp blonde hair and thoughtful gray eyes. That was Katie.

The other was a huge fat girl with a beard. Quinn took one look at the reflection, let out a shrill scream, and collapsed in a dead faint.

Chapter Five

"**K**atie! Jamie! I'm home."

"Oh, no! It's Mom." Katie knelt beside Quinn, who lay spread-eagled on the carpet, and tugged at her arm. "Come on. You've got to hide."

"You kids come help me with the groceries!" Mrs. Rolfing shouted from the garage door.

Quinn didn't budge. Katie slapped her pudgy cheeks several times. "Quinn! Get up!"

"Where am I?" Quinn mumbled.

"*Who* are you, is more like it," Katie shot back. She tucked her hands under her friend's arms and tried to pull Quinn to her feet. "Oomph! You weigh a ton."

Quinn promptly burst into tears and fell back onto the carpet. "Katie, what's happened to me?" she blubbered. "I've turned into a big old pig." She covered her face with her hand and wailed, "With a beard!"

"Kids!" Mrs. Rolfing yelled even more loudly. "Katie? Are you here?"

Katie was panic-stricken. "Look, Quinn, any second now my mother is going to walk into the house, see the kitchen and the dining room, and ground me for life. And she won't even notice whether you've put on a few pounds or have a beard."

Still whimpering, Quinn rolled onto her hands and knees. With a loud groan she heaved herself to her feet. "What should we do?"

"Let's hide in my room."

The two girls hurried down the hall toward the bedrooms. Katie motioned for Quinn to sit on the bed while she stood guard at the door. "I just need a little time," she whispered, "to figure out some answers."

"How could this happen to me?" Quinn asked, picking up a hand mirror from Katie's dresser.

"I don't know," Katie replied. "But I think it definitely has something to do with the carnival last night."

At the mention of the word, Quinn dropped the mirror, which shattered against the end table.

"Oh, no," Katie groaned. "More bad luck." Before she could pick up the bits of broken glass, an anguished shriek came from the kitchen.

Katie winced. "Mom found the mess. Now,

Quinn, be very quiet and maybe she won't guess that we're here."

Quinn didn't respond. She sat silently on the edge of the bed, her chubby cheeks stained with tears. Katie waved a hand in front of her friend's eyes.

"Quinn? Are you in there?"

Quinn stared blankly off into space.

Katie threw up her hands in despair. "Oh great. Now you've gone off to never-never land. Who *knows* what's going to happen when you come back."

"This is just terrible," Katie heard her mother's voice echo down the hall. "Jamie and his friends have gone too far. Well, that's it. No more snacks. No more free lunches. No more nothing."

Katie chewed her lip nervously. "Uh-oh. She's blaming my brother. Now Jamie'll get in trouble and come get me. Things are getting worse by the second."

Quinn suddenly sprang back to life. "The funhouse," she rasped. "It did this to me."

"Now we're getting somewhere." Katie kicked her bedroom door shut and perched on the bed. "While you were in there, did you eat anything strange?"

"I — I'm not sure," Quinn said uncertainly. "Maybe."

"Then maybe that's it."

"Food?"

41

"Sure," Katie said. "Bad food can cause you to, um . . . " She paused, struggling to find the right word to describe Quinn's sudden fatness. "Bloat."

"And grow a beard?" Quinn's chin quivered dangerously, signaling another downpour of tears.

"Maybe." Katie tried to sound encouraging. "If some drug, or something, was put in it, I bet anything could happen."

"You mean, all we have to do is find out what it was that we ate in the funhouse?" Quinn rubbed a pudgy fist into her eye and sniffled. "And then everything would be okay?"

Katie nodded vigorously. "Then we could tell a doctor about it and he or she could fix you."

Quinn brightened at that thought. "You really think that's possible?"

"Sure." Katie patted her on the back. "They have shots and pills that can make your symptoms go away instantly."

"Oh, Katie!" Quinn lumbered to her feet. "Then there isn't a moment to lose."

"Great!" Katie hurried to her door and listened in the hall. "It sounds like my mom's in the garage getting the groceries. If you go now, you can hurry out the front door, make a run for the fairgrounds, and Mom'll never know you were here."

"Me?" Quinn looked horrified. "I can't go outside."

"Why not?"

"Look at me!" Quinn stared down at her immense thighs that appeared to have doubled in size in the time they'd been hiding in the room. Her chin began to tremble once again. "I can't go anywhere looking like this. It's too awful."

"Then we'll just have to find someone else," Katie said, pacing the room. "Skip and Trevor are out. Skip's having some sort of growth spurt, and Trevor . . . well, I can't get anyone at his house to answer the door."

Quinn grabbed Katie's arm. "How about you?"

"Me?" Katie shot her friend a startled look. "Why me?"

"Because you're the only one left."

"Yeah, but . . ."

Quinn stared hard in Katie's eyes. "Don't tell me you're scared."

"Of course not," Katie protested, a little too loudly. "I just don't see why I have to do it."

"Because you're the only one left," Quinn repeated.

Katie was stumped. She absolutely, positively did not want to go anywhere near that funhouse again. "Well, what are you going to do while I go back to the carnival?" she hedged.

"I'll wait for you here."

Katie shook her head. "My mom'll find you and she'll get upset."

"She won't find me." Quinn whispered back. "I'll hide in your closet."

"But — "

"Just *go*."

Quinn shoved Katie toward the door. The movement made the side seam of Quinn's purple shirt rip open and she burst into tears.

"Oh, Katie," she moaned. "I'm getting bigger by the second."

Katie felt terrible. Quinn was miserable and scared and Katie knew it was her absolute duty to help.

"Don't cry," Katie pleaded, giving her friend's shoulders a squeeze. "I'll help you. I promise."

Quinn mustered a grateful smile. Then the garage door slammed and Katie hissed, "But remember, you have to hide. And don't make a sound."

Quinn nodded solemnly, then half-limped, half-waddled to the closet. "Please hurry, Katie," she said as she stepped inside. "Before it's too late."

Katie snatched a pillow off her bed, a couple of books from her bookshelf and a candy bar she'd hidden away in her sock drawer. "Here, take these," she said. "They'll make you more comfortable."

Quinn ignored the pillow and books but grabbed the candy bar and shoved it in her mouth, wrapper and all. A little stream of brown saliva dribbled out of the corner of Quinn's mouth as she chewed hungrily. "Thanks, Katie," Quinn mumbled, "you're a true friend."

"Take care!" Katie whispered cheerfully. "And don't worry — I'll be right back."

The moment Katie shut the closet door, she clutched her stomach. She felt like throwing up — partly from the shock of watching her best friend turn into a gross pig, but mostly from fear of returning to the funhouse. Katie forced herself to take a deep breath, then slipped out of her bedroom and tiptoed down the hall.

As she headed for the front door Katie could hear Mrs. Rolfing in the kitchen, talking to herself as she tried to clean up the mess. "Jamie is grounded, and I'm calling his friends' mothers to make sure they ground them, too."

Katie felt a little guilty letting her brother take the blame for Quinn's mess but she didn't have time to explain. Quinn seemed to be expanding by the second. If Katie didn't hurry and find out what was causing her friend's weight gain, Quinn might explode.

Katie found her bike lying on its side by the

front porch. She figured if she cut through the gully behind Woodrow Wilson Middle School and crossed the highway by the old fire station, it would take her ten minutes to reach the fairgrounds.

She leapt onto the seat and pedaled toward the carnival for all she was worth. As she rode, Katie went over her plan of action in her head. "Get in. Find out what happened to Quinn. Get out. Go home."

It sounded simple enough. It wasn't.

Chapter Six

No one was manning the ticket booth at the gate to the fairgrounds. In fact, the entire carnival looked deserted. The roller coaster and Ferris wheel towered above the kiddie rides like huge gray skeletons on the verge of collapse.

Katie slowly got off her bike and wheeled it through the metal turnstiles. Once inside she called in a tiny voice, "Hello? Is anybody here?"

Silence. Katie slowly guided her bike between the rows of game booths. Each had a locked metal grate pulled down in front of it. The stuffed Road Runners, Wile E. Coyotes, and Ninja Turtles peeking through the bars looked like prisoners in a stockade. Katie couldn't shake the feeling that all of them were watching her.

The only sound Katie heard as she walked was the crunch of the front wheel of her bike on the empty popcorn boxes and candy wrappers littering the ground.

Suddenly she glimpsed a movement out of the corner of her eye. Katie spun and faced the direction she thought it had come from.

A sign hanging from chains above the hot dog wagon swung back and forth.

"It's just the breeze, you scaredy-cat," she scolded herself. "Stop being so jumpy."

Katie ducked her head and continued moving through the carnival. She didn't stop at the Bullet, or the Scrambler, or any of the other rides. She knew exactly which part of the carnival had caused Quinn's problem and it took every ounce of her courage to keep moving toward it.

It happened again! Something was moving under the yellow canvas covering the mini boat ride. This time it wasn't her imagination. The movement intensified until the whole canvas shook. Katie was about to cry out in alarm when a chubby squirrel popped its nose out and cocked its head at her.

"You scared me half to death, you silly," Katie scolded the furry animal. "I nearly — "

Katie didn't finish her sentence. She'd caught sight of Greywold's Phantasmagoria looming out of the shadows behind the green building that housed the rest rooms.

In the fading light, the old wooden building

looked more rundown than ever. The roof sagged slightly in the middle and the painted signs on its sides were so faded, they were hardly visible.

"I'm surprised it hasn't been condemned," Katie mumbled as she raised her chin to look at the sign above the funhouse entrance.

"Oh!" she gasped.

It was the painting of Greywold the Magician. *He* was the one who had been watching her!

"That's impossible!" Katie said loudly, as if the volume of her voice would make it not so. But it was. The night before his yellow eyes had been watching as her friends entered through the lighted entrance. Today, those same eyes had narrowed to little slits and a scowl twisted the cruel smile painted on the magician's face.

"Nothing's impossible," a tiny voice declared.

Katie spun around and demanded shakily, "Who said that?"

"Me, myself, and I," came the high-pitched reply, followed by the hiccuping giggle of a little child's laugh.

The voice was coming from under the funhouse. Katie bent forward and peered into the shadows by the stairs. A small boy clad in knickers, a collarless white shirt, and a knit sweater vest crouched in the dirt.

"Who are you?" Katie demanded.

"Tommy Tippee. Tommy Tom-Tom. Tommy Boy," the sandy-haired child answered in a sing-song voice.

"Come out from there," Katie said.

"I couldn't possibly." Tommy answered. "I stay in the dark-dark. It's nice here. You come see."

Katie wheeled her bike up to the funhouse, put down the kickstand, and knelt in the dirt. The boy, who looked about six, grinned at her, revealing a big gap in his teeth. "Go on in."

"What are you talking about?"

"The funny-fun funhouse. That's what you came to see to see. Isn't it?"

"Well, uh, yes," Katie said. "But the carnival isn't open yet. There's no one to take my ticket."

Tommy held out a small dirty hand. "I'll take it. Gimmee-gimmee."

"But I don't have a ticket."

The boy shrugged and wrapped his hands around his knees. "Then I guess you don't need one. Go in."

There was something about the little boy that didn't look right. His clothes were rather old-fashioned. But it was his eyes that disturbed Katie most. They weren't angry. They weren't sad. They stared at Katie with no emotion at all.

"Are you with someone?" Katie asked, looking around for Tommy's parents.

"Nope. It's just me, myself, and I."

"Are you with the carnival?"

He cocked his head. "Isn't everyone?"

"Not me," Katie said.

"But you will be. You will be, you willy-willy-will be," he sang to himself. Then Tommy looked up at Katie and grinned. "Go in the funhouse. Have some fun."

"You come with me." Katie reached into the shadows to take his hand. The boy sprang backward just out of reach.

"No, no, no," he scolded. "Mustn't touch."

Katie straightened up. "Well, I'm not going into that rat trap alone."

"Don't worry. I'll be right here." The little boy's eyes widened slightly. "Watching."

"But what about the guard?" Katie looked over her shoulder in spite of herself. "What if I get caught?"

The boy named Tommy was drawing circles in the dirt with a stick. "Sooner or later we all get caught." He gestured with the stick to the front entrance. "Go on. Have some funny-fun-fun."

Katie looked up at the entrance and squared her shoulders. Every instinct in her body told her to go home. But Katie knew she had to go inside. Wasn't that the reason she'd come here, anyway? The funhouse held the answer to what had gone wrong with Quinn. Katie knew she had no choice but to enter.

"All right, Tommy, or whatever your name is," she muttered to the strange little boy as she walked toward the archway. "I'll go in."

As her foot crossed the threshold, she was greeted by a loud buzzer, followed by high-pitched maniacal laughter that echoed through the darkened interior. Katie swallowed hard.

"I just hope I come out."

Chapter Seven

"Hey, diddle diddle
The cat broke the fiddle
A cloud has covered the moon.
Don't ever laugh when you see such sport
Or you'll be crying soon."

A huge jack-in-the-box sprang out of the floor in the first chamber and leered at Katie. She shrieked and leapt sideways into the outstretched arms of a waxwork ballerina dressed in a long tutu and ballet slippers. Her face was frozen in a sad smile. For just the tiniest moment, Katie thought she felt the ballerina's fingers close around her shoulders.

"Yikes!"

Katie jerked away from the wax figure, making sure she didn't collide with anything else. The first chamber was lined with the wax dummies of a cowboy, a veiled belly dancer, a midget in a top hat and tails, and a Native American with a full-feathered headdress and buckskin leggings. They were so lifelike that Katie half imagined she saw them breathing. She hurried to the tiny door at the end of the room, which was the only way out.

"Come in, come in!" an eerie voice whispered from a dusty speaker hanging on a nail above the small door.

Katie dropped to her knees, opened the door, and crawled into a narrow tunnel lined with a complete miniature village. Little cars and trucks traveled back and forth between small white houses on either side of her. As she crawled along the tunnel, Katie saw several faces pressed against the windows of the little houses. They weren't happy faces.

"Help me! Help me!"

Katie cocked her head. Was that really a voice calling to her, or just the creak of the mechanical cars as they moved along their tracks? Before she could determine what was being said and where the voice was coming from, the tunnel came to an end.

Katie found herself in an elaborate Victorian sitting room covered with thick red brocade wallpaper.

The room looked like a museum gone mad. The walls were crooked, with everything out of proportion. Overstuffed armchairs fit for a giant sat beside cherrywood sideboards that only a child could have used. Dozens of oil portraits bordered by ornate wooden frames hung every which way on the walls.

The shifting perspective made Katie dizzy. As she tried to stand up, she fell against the dusty red wallpaper, knocking an oil painting of a family of redheaded people. She reached out to straighten the portrait but stopped short when she saw the eyes of one of the people in the picture, a man with a handlebar mustache, follow the movement of her hand. His gaze shifted to her face and Katie saw such fear in his eyes that she had to bite her lip to keep from screaming.

The room abruptly tilted and then spun completely around. A door at the far side of the room creaked open. Katie dove for it, yelling, "Get me out of here!"

Suddenly she was in another long hallway. Katie took a step forward and unseen cobwebs clung to her face. "Ick! Ick! Ick!" She flailed at her face and shoulders with her hands, struggling to pull the sticky strings off her skin.

"I want out!" Katie shouted, hoping Tommy would hear her. "This isn't fun at all."

Mocking laughter met her plea. At first Katie thought it was coming from just one person but the echoes spread up and down the corridor until it sounded like a crowd of people jeering at her. She tried to run but the floor beneath her feet turned into wooden rollers.

"Whoa!" Katie teetered back and forth like a lumberjack in a logrolling contest.

Just as abruptly the rollers stopped. Before Katie could catch her breath, she was hit by a blast of hot air from the floor that lifted her hair straight above her head. At the same time, a foghorn blasted in her ear. It was too much to bear. All at once she couldn't think of a single reason for staying in the funhouse. She'd found many strange, terrifying things, but no explanation at all for what had happened to Quinn. It was time to leave.

"Let me out!" she screamed, banging on a black wall of the tunnel. "Do you hear? I want out!"

The solid wall she had been hitting with her fist burst with a loud pop, like a balloon, and Katie fell through into the strangest room of all.

The air there was deathly cold. Wisps of blue fog floated in the corners. Heavy wooden frames lined the walls. Encased in each was a full length mirror. Katie stared mesmerized at the nearest mirror. As she watched, her own image seemed to shimmer and change. Her thin blonde hair grew dark and full, her clear blue eyes clouded to a dull brown, and a network of hideous scars crisscrossed her pale freckled skin.

"Oh, no!" Katie's hand flew to her face. "What's happening to me?"

"Don't look, girl!" a brittle old voice crackled in her ear. "Close your eyes."

Katie spun and found herself face to face with the old fortune teller. "What are you doing here?" Katie demanded.

"There's no time to explain," Annie Entwhistle replied. She motioned with her cane toward the door. "Come away from the mirror and leave this room this instant. You should never have gotten in here."

Katie tried to run but tripped on her shoelace. She tumbled onto the floor in front of three more mirrors. As she pulled herself to her feet, Katie saw her reflection change into the blurry outline of someone familiar, a person with warm brown skin and glasses. He seemed frozen in place with his arms outstretched.

"Trevor!" Katie screamed just as a clawlike hand folded around her arm and yanked her out of the funhouse.

"I told you not to look," Annie Entwhistle muttered as she dragged Katie toward her tent. "And I meant it."

"Owww!" Katie whimpered. "You're hurting me."

"Instead of crying, girl, you should be thanking me." The old lady pushed open her tent flap and shoved Katie inside. "Annie Entwhistle just saved your life."

Katie stumbled blindly into the dimly lit space. Once more her nostrils were filled with the smell of burning incense.

"Sit down, girl, and let Annie fix you a cup of tea." The old lady hobbled to the other side of the tent, where a two-burner hot plate rested on an old metal table. She picked up a black cast-iron tea kettle and set it on a burner. "It'll warm you up."

"I'm not cold." Katie's body was shaking so violently that her teeth chattered but it wasn't from the temperature. It was from fear.

"Well, sit down anyway," Annie said.

"I — I can't," Katie stammered. "I have to get away."

She stepped shakily toward the tent opening but Annie Entwhistle sprang forward with surprising agility and blocked her way. The fortune teller stretched her arms out to the sides.

"What about your friend? I thought you came here to help her."

Katie's knees locked. Annie really was a fortune teller. She slowly returned to the table and slipped into the chair. "What do you know about my friend?" Katie whispered.

Annie leaned in close to Katie and grinned. "You tell me what you know, and I'll return the favor."

Katie took a deep shaky breath. "My friend Quinn went in the funhouse last night and hasn't been the same since. She's huge. She's eating everything that isn't nailed down and getting bigger by the second. But weirdest of all — she's growing a beard."

Annie's cloudy gray eyes suddenly brightened. "Hmm . . . it sounds like she's transforming."

"What does that mean?" Katie demanded.

"Changing." Annie waved her hand at Katie. "It was an accident. Unplanned and unfortunate but there's nothing you can do about it."

Katie sprang to her feet. "There is, too. I can go get help. I should have done it in the first place."

"Just forget about your friend," Annie said emphatically. "Put her out of your head, girl."

"I can't. Because it's not just Quinn. Something's happened to Skip and Trevor, too. Skip's having some sort of growth spurt and I think I saw Trevor's reflection in that awful room full of mirrors. It looked like he was reaching out to me, like he needed my help."

Annie Entwhistle reached across the table and clutched Katie's chin in her hand. The pupils of her eyes were huge and black. "Listen to me, and listen good," she said. "Greater forces than you could ever imagine are working against you."

Katie stared into the old woman's eyes and whispered, "Who *are* you people?"

Annie released Katie's chin and sank back in her chair. "We are all that remains of Greywold's Traveling Phantasmagoria." She gestured at the framed photographs strung across the canvas walls of the tent.

"Who's Greywold?" Katie asked.

"The greatest magician who ever lived," Annie replied.

Katie got up to take a closer look at one of the yellowing photographs. A man in a black cape and top hat stood in the shade of a big striped tent. His face was obscured by the shadows but as she studied the picture little goose bumps crept up Katie's arm.

Katie quickly moved on to the next picture. A muscular man in white tights, satin shorts, and a striped tank top flexed his biceps toward the camera. On one arm sat a small boy. A pretty woman dressed like a gypsy balanced on the other. Behind them stood an immense lady with a paper fan covering her face. In the background, two men, one very large and the other no taller than a child, stood smoking cigarettes, their backs turned to the camera. There was something familiar about all of them but Katie couldn't put her finger on it.

"Those people look like ordinary circus performers," Katie murmured, as she peered at a wide photo filled with white-faced clowns, acrobatic midgets, and plumed ladies in sequined tights.

"Oh, Greywold's Phantasmagoria was anything but ordinary," Annie Entwhistle hissed. "It was the greatest carnival on earth, with trained animals and performers that would shock and amaze you."

"What happened?"

Annie shrugged. "One dark, awful night Greywold changed. Soon everything else did, too. The animals died. The performers disappeared one by one, no one knew where. We'd wake up to find them gone. The games and rides were closed down. Finally all that remained was his cursed funhouse."

"Cursed?" Katie swallowed hard. "You mean, like someone put a spell on it?"

The old lady took a drink of her tea. She stared long and hard at Katie but said nothing.

"Why?" Katie breathed softly. "And how?"

Suddenly the wind kicked up, making the sides of the old canvas tent flap against each other. The candle on the table flickered violently, casting deep shadows into the thin pool of light. Annie sat frozen, with her cup halfway to her lips. Finally she said, "He's here."

"Who?" Katie's voice rose shrilly. "Why won't you answer my questions?"

"There isn't time." The old woman slammed her cup into the saucer and gripped Katie's shoulders. "Leave these grounds and *never* come back. Try never to think of us again."

"But my friends — "

"Forget them." Annie Entwhistle rose to her feet and backed nervously into the shadows of her tent. "They're trapped. Changed forever." She looked fearfully toward the tent door, as if she expected something horrible to appear there any second. "Now go! Begone with you!"

Katie needed no encouragement. Her chair fell back against the table as she bolted into the late afternoon light.

Outside, the carnival was just coming to life. The Bullet, filled with its first load of riders, was inching into the air. Then the cars descended and thrilled screams rang across the clear sky, mingling with the calliope music from the carousel.

Everything was so cheerful and wholesome. Standing by the ring toss were Mr. and Mrs. Hendricks, watching their son Elliot try to win a stuffed alligator. Katie had known the Hendrickses all her life. They lived just down the street from her. Looking up and down the midway she saw more and more neighbors and friends that she knew from Wheaton. She turned and looked back at the funhouse. Seen from the outside, it looked like a drab little carnival sideshow. Hardly the nightmarish place she had just escaped from.

In fact, with each passing minute, her bizarre visit to the funhouse and her strange encounter with old Annie Entwhistle grew less real in her mind.

"It's just like me," Katie muttered, "to blow everything out of proportion. Quinn and the others are probably playing some big joke on me.

People don't suddenly get fat and grow beards overnight. And dilapidated old funhouses in two-bit carnivals don't have any magical powers."

Katie had almost convinced herself that she had just imagined seeing Trevor's image in that mirror when she caught sight of the strange little boy standing in the arched entrance of the funhouse.

He was half in shadow, the light falling on his upturned face. He smiled at Katie, an open, innocent smile that bore no trace of guile. She found herself smiling back. He gestured slightly for her to come toward him. Katie stepped forward without thinking. Then she stopped in her tracks.

The boy was not alone. A tiny flash of brilliant red light glittered near his head. It took Katie a second to identify its source — a large ruby ring on a black-gloved hand. Someone was standing beside the boy, completely hidden in the shadows, holding the child's hand. But this was no ordinary human being. Katie was sure of that.

She turned on her heels and fled.

Chapter Eight

Katie was so upset by the carnival that she completely forgot about her bicycle and ran all the way home. As she ran, Katie couldn't shake the sensation of fingers brushing against the back of her neck. She hunched up her shoulders and ran faster.

When she got to her house, Katie tore through the front door, closed it, locked it, and even fastened the little security chain. Then she hurried through the den and locked the sliding door to the backyard, too. She slipped her brother Jamie's baseball bat into the sliding grooves so that even if someone broke the lock they wouldn't be able to open the door. After that, she collapsed face down on the living room carpet, completely out of breath.

"Katie, is that you?" she heard her mother call from one of the bedrooms down the hall.

"Yes, Mom," Katie huffed. "At least, I hope it's me."

An awful thought suddenly entered Katie's head. What if what had happened to Quinn had also happened to her? She crawled to the couch and pulled herself up to peer in the mirror above the fireplace.

The face she saw was a mess. Tiny rivulets of sweat streamed down her cheeks and damp strands of hair clung to her flushed skin.

"Thank goodness," Katie breathed, leaning her forehead against the mantel in relief. "It's still me."

"I want to talk to you, young lady," her mother called.

"Where are you?" Katie asked over her shoulder.

"In your room."

"*What?*"

Katie thought she'd spent every last bit of energy running home, but the thought that her mother might discover Quinn sent her racing into her bedroom. To her horror, she heard her mother's muffled voice coming from inside her closet.

"What a pigsty," Mrs. Rolfing complained. "How can you kids be such slobs? First I find empty food containers thrown all over the house. And now this."

"This?" Katie stuck her head inside the closet, half-expecting to see her bloated friend cowering behind the rack of dresses. Instead, she found all of her clothes dumped on the floor.

"Look." Her mother pointed to the wooden bar that supported the clothes hangers. It was split in two and lay on top of the pile of dresses. "What were you doing? Swinging on this?"

Katie shook her head. "Quinn must have pulled on it," she murmured. "And it couldn't hold her weight. But where did she go?"

Her mother blew a strand of hair off her forehead. "Now just a minute. First your brother blames the dog for garbage all over the house, and now you're blaming your best friend for this." Mrs. Rolfing picked up the broken pieces of wood and dumped them in the wastebasket by Katie's desk. "What's with you kids today, anyway?"

This was it. Either Katie took her mother into her confidence and told her the whole weird tale, or she kept quiet and tried to solve things herself. She decided she'd better talk to her mother.

"Uh, Mom?" Katie began, picking up the clothes off the floor. "If I tell you something so incredibly strange that it seems impossible, will you promise to believe me?"

"Katie, your dad and I are having a big party tomorrow night," her mother replied, "and I have to clean this entire house from top to bottom. I don't have time for riddles."

"It's not a riddle, Mom. It's a problem. A big problem. So will you just listen?"

Her mother blew the same wayward strand of hair off her forehead again and folded her arms across her chest. "Okay. I'm listening."

Katie bit her lip as she tried to think where to begin. "Last night I went to the carnival with Quinn, Skip, and Trevor — "

"On a school night and against my better judgment," Mrs. Rolfing cut in. "I had a terrible time trying to get you up this morning."

"Well, something happened there," Katie said, ignoring her mother's remark. "Something really bad."

"Oh, no," Mrs. Rolfing groaned, dropping her arms to her sides. "What did you do wrong?"

"Mother! I didn't do anything. Something happened to my friends. In the funhouse."

"Funhouse?" Mrs. Rolfing repeated, a frown creasing her brow.

Katie clasped her hands in her lap and stared down at them. "Somebody, or something, got them while they were inside and changed them."

"Changed them?" Mrs. Rolfing put her hands on her hips and asked, "What are you talking about?"

"Well one second Quinn was this skinny seventh-grader, and the next she'd put on two hundred pounds."

Mrs. Rolfing laughed. "Oh, now really, Katie, get serious."

"I am serious, Mom," Katie protested. "I think this funhouse is owned by someone who is a real magician and can do stuff like that."

"There's no such thing as a real magician," Mrs. Rolfing said. "They're just illusionists. Their tricks are all done with smoke and mirrors."

"Mirrors!" Katie repeated. "That's what Greywold used. Mirrors. And now that I think about it, the room did seem to be filled with a kind of a blue smoke."

Mrs. Rolfing nodded. "You see, illusionists use those devices to make rabbits *look* like they're disappearing into hats, and people *look* like they're being cut in half and, in Quinn's case, girls *look* like they've gained two hundred pounds."

"But, Mom, Quinn doesn't just *look* fat, she is fat."

Mrs. Rolfing rolled her eyes. "Oh, come on."

"You've got to believe me, Mom," Katie insisted. "Quinn's the one who devoured all the food in the kitchen. When you came home, she hid in the closet and must have broken the rod."

"Look, Katie," her mother interrupted, "just because your friend's gained a little weight, that's no reason to — "

"A little? Mother, she's a blimp! I'm surprised she was able to get out of that closet."

"I told you, I don't have time for your jokes,"

her mother scolded. "You've had your fun. Now let me get on with my cleaning."

"It's not just Quinn," Katie pleaded. "Skip's turned into some kind of strong man and Trevor is barking instead of speaking. I'm telling you, they're not themselves anymore."

"Are you all right?" Mrs. Rolfing put her hand on her daughter's forehead. "I think you've got a temperature. You feel awfully warm." She got up from the bed and hurried into the hall.

"That's because I nearly killed myself running away from the funhouse," Katie shouted after her mother.

"I don't want to hear another word about that funhouse. You're just being ridiculous." Katie could hear her mother ransacking the medicine chest in the bathroom in search of a thermometer.

"Mom, I'm trying to tell you that something really evil — "

Tap! Tap! Tap!

Katie's words caught in her throat as she spied an enormous face at her bedroom window. It had a huge forehead, big bulging eyes, and a curly red mustache — and it was calling her name!

"Katie!" the familiar voice said in a hoarse whisper. "Don't tell your mom anything!"

"Skip?" Katie leaned toward the window, peering into the darkness. "Is that really you?"

"Yes," Skip moaned. "All seven feet of me."

"Oh, my gosh!" Katie staggered backward. "You're a giant!"

"Katie, I'm going to check the medicine chest in our bathroom!" Mrs. Rolfing shouted from the hall. "I want you to lie down right now."

Katie wanted to yell for help but all she could croak was a feeble, "Mom?"

Skip pressed his huge face against the glass and mouthed, "Please don't tell!"

"Okay, Mom," Katie called back. "I'm uh, lying down." Then she inched cautiously up to the window. "Skip! What's happening to everyone?"

"I don't know. I just keep getting taller and taller." He ran a big beefy hand across the fringe of red hair ringing his bald head. "And my hair keeps getting longer — what's left of it."

Katie slowly raised her window to get a better look at her friend. People often described Skip as being short and sturdy. Now he looked like the wrestler Hulk Hogan. He was wearing a pair of his father's sweatpants and T-shirt, which looked like tight shorts and a midriff shirt on Skip.

"I can't believe it's you," she whispered. "It's just incredible."

"It's terrible," Skip moaned. "Katie, I'm really scared."

"Quinn's changed, too," Katie said, leaning out into the evening air.

"Did she get tall?"

"No," Katie shook her head. "Fat."

"Fat?" Skip's eyes widened. "Perfect Quinn?"

"And not only fat," Katie added. "But she grew a *beard*."

"A bearded fat lady," Skip repeated, shaking his head slowly. "What about Trevor? Is he okay?"

Katie shrugged helplessly. "I don't know. I went to his house, but he wouldn't answer the door. Then I went back to the funhouse — "

"Wait a minute," Skip cut in. "You went back to that place by yourself?"

Katie nodded. "I know it's hard to believe, but Quinn begged me to go. She thought I'd be able to find a solution to your, uh, problem."

"What did you find?"

"At first I thought maybe you guys had been given something to make you change, but I didn't see anything. Just really scary images and . . . and those mirrors."

"Mirrors!" Skip pressed the palms of his hands against his temples. "Terrible mirrors," he gasped. "Stay away!" He thrust his hand forward and Katie heard a loud crunch in the wall.

"Skip!" Katie whispered. "What happened?"

Skip leaned his head against the side of her house and moaned, "I just punched a hole in the side of your house. I'm really sorry."

"Boy, you are strong!" Katie marveled. "That's brand-new aluminum siding."

Skip turned his head to look at her. "I don't know what's going on, Katie, or what to do."

"Have your parents seen you?"

"They're off playing tennis. I left them a note that I was going out to the carnival and then spending the night at Trevor's house. I didn't want them to worry."

"I tried to talk to my mom but she thought I was delirious." Katie took a deep breath. "I think we need to call the police."

"No!" Skip bellowed. "If they see me, they'll put me in the hospital and by the time the doctors figure out what's happened to this body" — he paused and stared off into the distance — "the carnival will have left town."

"I found the thermometer!" Mrs. Rolfing called from the master bathroom.

"Oh, darn." Katie leaned out the window and whispered hurriedly, "We've got to find Quinn and Trevor right way. Maybe the three of us can come up with a way to solve this thing together."

"Maybe." Skip sounded very doubtful. He backed into the shadows of Katie's yard. "But time's running out. I can feel it."

"Skip, don't go anywhere." Katie heard her mother's footsteps just outside her room. "Wait for me, okay? I'll be right out."

She quickly closed the window and dove under the covers just as her mother came through her door. Katie shut her eyes and pretended to be asleep.

Mrs. Rolfing set a glass on the bedside table and sighed. "Sleep is the best thing for you, honey." She tucked the blue-and-white quilt up under Katie's chin. "All this talk about fun-houses and magicians. You must have been delirious."

Katie felt the gentle press of lips against her forehead. Then she listened to her mother's footsteps pad out of her bedroom and the door being shut behind her.

It was agony, but Katie forced herself to wait a full fifteen minutes before getting up. She knew that every passing minute meant more terrible things could be happening to Skip and Quinn. She dared not even think about what was going on with Trevor.

Finally, at exactly 9:02, Katie hopped out of bed. She stuffed pillows under the covers and grabbed a jacket from the floor of her closet. She glanced out the window to see if by some miracle Skip had waited for her. But there was no sign of him.

As she climbed onto the windowsill, Katie caught a glimpse of her reflection in the dresser mirror. She barely recognized herself. A day ago, Katie had been the biggest scaredy-cat at

Woodrow Wilson Middle School, afraid to go on even the mildest rides at the carnival. Now she was sneaking out of her house in the middle of the night to chase after giants and bearded fat people.

"Here goes nothing." Katie took a deep breath and leapt off the sill into the darkness.

Chapter Nine

*"Three blind mice, three blind mice,
See how they run, see how they run."*

Katie crouched low by her back hedge. She had searched all over her backyard for Skip but he was nowhere to be found. Now a girl was singing in a familiar, off-key voice somewhere close by.

She followed the voice like a beacon to the abandoned toolshed in the backyard of the old Grafton house. Katie and her friends had often used it as a secret clubhouse when they were younger.

"Quinn?" Katie whispered at the metal door of the rusty tin shack.

"Oh, Katie, you found me," Quinn gasped from inside. "I was afraid I was going to have to spend the rest of my life in here."

"Why did you leave my closet?"

"I just kept getting bigger and bigger," she moaned. "And it scared me. So I waited till your mom went back to the garage and then I ran."

"How'd you end up in here?"

"Your dog, Britty, saw me and didn't recognize me. She chased me here."

"Well, Britty's inside now and no one can see you, so you can come out."

"No, I can't," Quinn whimpered. "I'm stuck."

"Hold on. I'll get you out."

Katie unlatched the door to the toolshed and it creaked loudly as it opened. She didn't dare turn on the light for fear that her parents might see it and wonder what was going on. She groped with her hand for a small flashlight that had always been stored on a shelf to the right of the door.

"They all ran after the farmer's wife,
Who cut off their tails with — "

"Quinn, cut the singing," Katie warned. "My parents might hear you."

"If I don't sing, I start to think about what's happening to me and then I get really scared."

Katie found the flashlight and flipped the switch on its side with her thumb. Nothing happened.

"Well don't sing so loud, it hurts my ears," Katie kidded as she banged the flashlight against her hand to get it to work.

"How can you joke at a time like this?" Quinn said in a hurt voice.

"To keep from crying," Katie shot back. "This

whole thing is like a bad dream. I mean, you should see what's happened to — *aaaghhh!*"

The flashlight popped on and its beam lit Quinn like a spotlight. She was enormous. Katie guessed Quinn weighed at least three hundred pounds now. Quinn had draped herself in a large rain poncho from the top of Katie's closet.

Tears spilled from Quinn's tiny eyes down her big broad cheeks into her thick beard. "Am I that awful looking?"

"N-n-no," Katie stammered. "It's just a little, um, shocking. I mean, when you said you were stuck, I thought you meant your foot was caught in some fencing wire, or the lawn mower handle, or something like that. I had no idea your whole body would be wedged in here."

"Don't say it like that," Quinn groaned. "I feel bad enough as it is."

"Well, don't panic, I'll get you out." Katie clambered over some shovels and tugged at a wheelbarrow and a few old bicycles that were hemming Quinn in. "If I just shove these out of the way, maybe we can — "

A shadow loomed across the open door and Katie's heart fluttered in her chest. Then a voice she knew well exclaimed, "I thought *I* was cursed! You're a disaster."

Katie aimed her flashlight at the doorway. The light revealed two long legs and part of a trunk of a huge man. Skip was taller than the shed and had to bend sideways to look inside.

Quinn's jaw fell open. "Skip! You're tall — and ugly!"

"And you're the Goodyear blimp." Skip ducked under the door frame and stared at Quinn in amazement. "Boy, when you sit around the house, you sit *around* the house."

Quinn narrowed her beady eyes at him. "That's so funny I forgot to laugh."

Katie pinched herself on the arm in the faint hope that she was just having a dream and would soon wake up. But it was no dream. She really was watching an oversized muscleman and a gigantic bearded lady bicker. And they were her friends.

"Skip, where were you?" Katie hissed. "I looked all over for you."

"I went to find Trevor but had to hide." Skip lowered his voice to barely a whisper. "Someone was following me."

"Help me, please," a new voice called softly into the shed. Skip straightened up so fast he banged his head on the ceiling. Quinn squealed with fright and Katie stumbled backward into the rake handles.

"Don't panic. It's me, Trevor."

Katie shone her light out the door again. Hunched in the doorsill was a very tiny person no more than three feet tall. He wore a trench coat that dragged behind him on the ground, a big slouch hat that covered most of his face, and thick, dark glasses.

"Trevor?" Skip repeated, incredulously.

"Not so loud, Skip," Trevor warned, looking nervously over his shoulder. "He might hear you."

"He who?" Katie demanded.

Trevor threw his arms in the air. "The man who's after me. Now would you let me in, before it's too late?" Before any of them could refuse, Trevor hopped over the sill and shut the shed door behind him. "Shhh! Don't move. Don't even breathe."

Trevor froze in place, his head pressed against the metal door. All four of them stayed very still, listening intently. Suddenly they heard the *swish-swish* of feet moving through the grass outside. The steps stopped and Katie felt her heart stop with them. Then, after what seemed like an eternity, the steps began again. They faded away into the distance and Trevor exhaled a sigh of relief.

"I think he's gone." Trevor tugged on the leg of Katie's jeans. "Would you check just to make sure?"

Katie focused her flashlight on Trevor's face and asked, "Trev? Is that really you?"

Trevor removed his hat and glasses, revealing the same doglike face she'd seen in his bedroom window. "I'm afraid so," he said sadly.

Skip bent from the waist and peered into Trevor's face. "Whoa! You look like a cross between E.T. and Benji."

Trevor reached up and tweaked Skip's bulbous nose. "And you look like the Incredible Hulk."

"No," Quinn blubbered from the corner, "that's me."

"Now, Quinn, don't cry," Katie chastened, turning the beam of her flashlight on the big, round girl. "It doesn't help anything."

Trevor got his first clear view of Quinn and he gasped, "You're like the famous bearded fat lady from the sideshow."

"Freak show, is more like it," Skip muttered.

"Freak show?" Katie gasped. "Is that what you said?"

Skip nodded. "Yeah. What about it?"

"What about it?" Katie trained her light on Quinn. "Don't you remember the sign you pointed to last night?"

Quinn nibbled on the side of her fingernail as she thought. "It's vague, but I think I remember."

"What was painted on it?"

Quinn cocked her head. "Pictures from another time. Little striped tents standing side by side."

"Uh-huh," Katie said encouragingly. "And what was on the banner that ran across the top of those tents?"

"Freak show," Trevor blurted out.

Katie nodded. "And whose pictures were on the billboards out front?"

"A strong man, a fat lady, and . . ." Skip turned slowly to look at Trevor. "Someone they called the dog-faced boy."

"*Dog*-faced!" Trevor repeated indignantly. "I don't look at all like a dog. Do I, Katie?"

Katie stared at Trevor, trying not to wince. "Well, maybe a bulldog . . . or one of those really wrinkled Sharpeis. But that's all."

"Oh, this is terrible." Trevor covered his face with his hands. "Just terrible."

"Maybe not," Katie said, patting him on the shoulder. "I think we've made a very important discovery. The three of you look exactly like those freaks in that painting of Greywold's Phantasmagoria."

"I don't think we just *look* like those freaks," Skip cut in. "I think we *are* those freaks."

"But how could that happen?" Quinn asked.

"I don't know," Skip replied. "But it has. I'm definitely as strong as an ox, Trevor's a dog-faced boy, and you've become a bearded fat lady."

Quinn could barely ask the next question. "Do you think I'm going to be trapped in this body forever?"

Her eyes welled up with tears and Katie pleaded, "Quinn, please don't cry. There's got to be a logical explanation for all of this."

"Oh, what do *you* know!" Quinn retorted, her

face growing redder by the second. "You're fine. You've got your own body." Quinn punched at her doughy body. "Where's mine?"

"And mine!" Skip straightened his seven-foot frame and hit his head on the ceiling again.

"And mine." Trevor hopped onto a rusted wheelbarrow and shook his tiny fists at Katie. "Where is it? Tell me."

Katie put her hands over her ears to shut out their accusing voices. "I think your own bodies are back at the funhouse," she yelled, "trapped in the Hall of Mirrors!"

"What?" They all stopped shouting.

"I thought I saw Trevor's body inside a mirror this afternoon," Katie explained. "And I'd be willing to bet that yours are there, too."

"That would mean that some sort of transfer must have happened last night in the funhouse," Trevor reasoned.

"When the lightning struck," Katie said, remembering the bolt of light that zigzagged across the sky.

"Lightning?" Skip repeated.

Katie nodded. "While you three were inside, I thought I saw lightning hit the funhouse, and then all of the lights went out."

Trevor scratched thoughtfully behind one ear. "It's all starting to come back to me. I remember being in some room with mannequins that seemed to be breathing."

Skip tugged on his moustache. "And I remember crawling through a tunnel filled with tiny people."

"And then I remember someone or something pulling me into an awful room filled with blue smoke," Quinn added. "And I knew I didn't want to be there."

"Was it the Hall of Mirrors?" Katie asked, shining her flashlight on their faces.

All three nodded.

"But these weren't regular mirrors," Trevor continued. "They had people inside. Lots of people, reaching out for us."

"I stood in front of one mirror," Quinn whispered. "And before I knew it I was being pulled through the glass by . . ." She paused and her eyes widened in surprise. "By a very large woman with a beard."

"That's right! Now I remember," Skip cut in excitedly. "A giant had a hold of me. I was almost into the mirror when . . . when something happened. There was a bright light, and a loud crash . . ."

"The lightning!" Trevor cried with glee.

Katie nodded with excitement. "And instead of the giant pulling you into the mirror, his body got stuck outside."

"And our bodies are stuck inside." Quinn looked down at herself and wailed, "I want my body back!"

Suddenly, an explosion like a shotgun blast shook the shed and the door was ripped off its hinges, falling onto the floor. Filling the doorsill was the tattooed man from the carnival.

"No one leaves the funhouse," he growled, "and lives to tell the tale!"

Chapter Ten

"Ive got me orders to bring you in!"
The tattooed man's eyes burned with a fierce red glow that Katie had seen only once before. That same light had shone from the ruby ring of the gloved hand in the shadows of the funhouse door.

"Come along, nice and quietlike," the bald-headed man hissed, "and there'll be no trouble." He focused his eyes on Skip and held out his hand. Skip stepped forward obediently, as if he were in a trance.

"Leave Skip alone," Katie shouted, "or I'm calling the police."

The man spun on Katie in a fury. He lifted one tattooed arm in front of her face and she cowered back, awaiting the blow. Then she realized that the tattooed dragon on his forearm was actually moving. It swished its tail back and forth, and puffed smoke from its nostrils.

While Katie watched, mesmerized, the man

spoke to the others. "Through the door and down the street. That's the way."

Frightening images swirled around Katie's head. She saw two-headed monsters gnashing their teeth at her. Ghostly figures with skeletal faces surrounded her, moaning her name. Her brother came up with outstretched arms to give her a hug. When she opened her arms to embrace him, his hands turned to fierce claws and he slashed at her face, laughing.

"No, no, no!" Katie shut her eyes and tried to drive the thoughts out of her head. Only something totally evil could play such terrible tricks on her mind. "Fight, everybody," she shouted, reaching for a shovel. "Don't look at his eyes or his tattoos. Don't let him get you!"

Trevor had gone catatonic while the bald man spoke. Suddenly he popped back to life and, snatching up a green lawn bag partially filled with grass clippings, sprang onto the man's back. He pulled the bag over the thug's head and screeched, "Fight is right! We're not going with you."

Katie swung desperately at the evil man's stomach with the rake. "Quinn, do something!"

"Let me at him!" Quinn swayed back and forth like an elephant, bouncing her huge girth against the sides of the tiny shed. With each shake it slipped further and further off of its foundation. "I'll squash him!"

Skip stood frozen as the shed rocked back and

forth around him. He seemed hypnotized with fear. Katie rapped the handle of the rake against Skip's shin, hard.

"Ouch!" Skip snapped out of his trance with a howl of pain. "What'd you have to go and do that for?"

Katie didn't explain. She pointed at the tattooed man and yelled, "Get him, Skip, before he gets us."

Skip looked around for a weapon, then decided to use his fist. He cocked his gigantic arm and ripped a punch deep into the man's belly. The man curled forward with a loud grunt, clutching his stomach as Quinn tore the shed off its foundation.

The entire structure collapsed sideways. A loose beam flew from the ceiling, knocking the tattooed man into the falling debris. With a tremendous heave, Skip shoved the shed the rest of the way over, so that the man was pinned beneath the debris.

"Don't let him up," Skip ordered Katie and the others. "Stand on the top of this mess."

Quinn spun around like a giant elephant and sat her immense bulk squarely on top of the fallen man.

"Get off me!" he cried. "Do ye hear? Get off!"

"Heads up!" Skip held an old picnic table in the air. "When I say three, run!"

"Where?" Katie asked.

"Anywhere," Skip replied. "Away from here.

One, two — " He tossed the table onto the wreckage of the shed, then roared, "Three!"

The four of them made a strange sight as they cut across the backyards of Wheaton. Katie was in the lead, followed by a loping giant and a furry gnome, who had to run twice as fast to keep up. Quinn brought up the rear. She had become as wide as she was tall and was rapidly falling behind.

"Please stop," Quinn begged after they'd run at least six blocks. She collapsed against the tree of a corner lot and huffed, "I can't run anymore. My chest hurts and I'm going to throw up."

Trevor flopped on the lawn next to Quinn. "I need to catch my breath, too."

Even Katie felt a sharp pain in her side. She dug her fist into her waist and bent sideways, wincing.

Skip was the only one who didn't seem winded. While he waited for the others to catch their breath, he asked, "What should we do now?"

"Get help," Quinn managed to choke out.

"Where?" Trevor asked between breaths. "Who would believe or help us?"

"No one," Katie said, pushing several strands of damp hair off her face. "We're on our own now." She took a deep breath. "And that means one thing."

"What?" Skip asked.

"We have to go back to the funhouse."

Quinn shook her head vigorously. "That's what he wants. That thug."

"She's right," Skip said. "The tattooed guy wanted to take us in. We can't go there. It'd be like surrendering."

"But don't you see," Katie pleaded. "That's where your bodies are. You *have* to go back."

"But what do we do when we get there?" Skip asked.

"I've got an idea," Trevor said suddenly. "But we have to break into Sliter's lumberyard to do it."

"Sliter's lumberyard?" Quinn repeated. "Have you lost your mind?"

"No." Trevor grinned slyly. "Found it. I'm going to make a lightning rod. And the supplies are at Sliter's."

"Lightning rod," Skip repeated. "You mean, like something that lightning will strike?"

Trevor held up his crossed fingers. "That's what I'm hoping."

"Why?" the other three chorused.

Trevor held up his hands for silence. "I'll explain on the way."

He led Katie and the others down the dark side streets paralleling Main, making sure they always kept to the shadows of the trees. "You see," he whispered, "in order to get our real bodies back, I figure we need to re-create the exact circumstances that happened when the transfer took place."

Katie's eyes widened. "So you want to make a lightning rod and put it on top of the funhouse!"

"Then the three of us will get in front of those mirrors," Trevor breathed excitedly. "And — "

"And do what?" Quinn cut in. "Stand there and wait for lightning to strike?" She raised one skeptical eyebrow. "Oh, puh-*leeze*."

"Trevor, the odds of lightning striking twice in one place are a million to one," Skip pointed out.

"But what were the odds of *this*" — Trevor gestured down at his tiny furry form — "happening to our bodies?"

"Probably ten trillion zillion to one," Skip replied.

"Exactly," Trevor answered. "And hey, you guys, I'm not crazy. Look up at the sky."

Katie did as she was told. To her surprise, she saw thick, dark clouds crossing the moon. The wind was picking up, making the leaves in the trees shudder above them. "I don't believe it. It looks like a storm's coming in. A bad one, too."

"Which is what you'd expect in the springtime when you live in Nebraska," Trevor said triumphantly. "Besides, these last twenty-four hours have been so strange that I believe anything can happen."

Skip nodded. "Before I left my house, I heard the weatherman say they've put Wheaton and all of the southern Nebraska counties on tornado watch."

Trevor clapped his tiny hands together. "Excellent news. Now let's get to work. We have to borrow a metal pole and some conducting wire."

"But hurry," Quinn said, peering back over her shoulder into the darkness. "I've got a feeling that we don't have much time."

When they reached the lumberyard, Trevor began to climb the fence but Katie whispered, "Wait a minute. The gate isn't locked."

She pushed on the gate and it opened with a loud creak. Trevor looked upward and said fervently, "Thank you, thank you, thank you!"

The lumberyard was crammed with tall stacks of boards covered in blue tarpaulins. A row of yellow forklifts sat silently in front of the entrance to the massive tin-roofed warehouse. A yellow safety light burned brightly above the door, casting long shadows over the piles of cement blocks and masonry supplies. Coils of metal fencing lay stacked against the walls of the warehouse.

They moved silently through the lumberyard, trying to find anything that looked like a metal pole.

"Two-by-fours, cedar shakes, shingles, rails, posts, paneling, wainscoting." Trevor listed off the items they passed.

"I hate to bring this up, Trevor," Skip said after they'd nearly circled the entire warehouse, "but how much do you really know about making a lightning rod?"

Trevor shrugged. "What's to know? It's simple enough. The process of making clouds can generate huge concentrations of electrically charged ions. They look for an opposite charge on the ground. Lightning's what you get when the positive and negative charges equalize."

"I just went brain dead," Katie groaned.

"It's like pressure in a dam," Trevor continued. "The charge is looking for something to let loose on. So we find a good conductor, like an iron rod, and stick it up there where the storm can see it. That's all."

Quinn shook her head. "I wish I'd paid closer attention in science class. This is very confusing."

"Don't worry. Our big problem is figuring out a way to direct the current to where we want it once it's struck the lightning rod."

"No, I'd say our problem is finding a metal rod," Skip said. "So far we haven't seen anything in this lumberyard but wood."

"My brother's Cub Scout troop just bought a big flagpole from this place," Trevor said. "I know they've got some, we just need to find them."

"Would you guys please hurry," Quinn moaned. "I have this feeling that we're being followed again."

"Just a minute," Katie gasped, as she caught

sight of something glinting in the moonlight. "What's that over there?"

Trevor grinned at her. "Flag pole sections, naturally." Suddenly the smile froze on his face. His lips barely moved as he whispered, "He's coming."

Even Katie could feel the evil chill. Goosebumps broke out on her legs and arms, and her mouth went dry. "What should we do? I'm scared."

"Me, too!" Quinn cried.

Skip hoisted a pack of four-foot-long metal rods over his shoulder. "Cut it out. If you get scared now, you'll never make it through the night," he said. "Now grab some wire and let's beat it."

They found a roll of baling wire and hurried out of the lumberyard into the back alley.

When they reached the highway, Katie and the others paused to listen for footsteps following them. Instead, they heard the tinny music of the carnival punctuated by a more distant, ominous sound.

"Thunder," Trevor whispered. "Music to my ears."

Chapter Eleven

"**O**h, drat!" Katie muttered as the foursome approached the dirt back lot of the fairgrounds. A man wearing an orange vest and a hat that read WHEATON 4-H was perched on a wooden sawhorse, guarding the back gate. "He'll never let us in."

"Not looking like this," Quinn muttered.

They ducked behind a dusty pickup for a quick huddle.

"How are we going to get inside?" Skip asked. "The carnival is completely surrounded by a chain link fence."

"We could go in the front gate but I don't have any money," Katie said. "How about you guys?"

All three shook their heads.

"We'll have to go over the top," Trevor said.

"I'm sure." Quinn folded her pudgy arms across her chest. "I can't climb over anything. Not with this body. I can barely walk."

Skip peeked around the side of the truck at the ten-foot tall fence. "I say we knock it down. With my strength and Quinn's weight — "

"Thanks a lot," Quinn mumbled.

"It'd be a cinch," Skip finished.

"Then everyone in the carnival would know we're here," Trevor said with a vigorous shake of his head. "That's a stupid idea."

"I'll tell you what's stupid," Skip shot back. "Standing around here chatting while a tattooed thug is after our lives!"

"Cut it out, you guys," Katie whispered. It was clear everyone's nerves were getting frayed. "The last thing we need is to get into a fight."

Trevor snapped his fingers. "I think I've got a solution."

"Let's hear it," Quinn said.

"First Skip throws the lightning rods over the fence onto the funhouse roof," Trevor said. "Then Katie and I climb up and install the lightning rod."

"What do we do while you're on the roof?" Skip asked.

"Stand guard," Trevor replied.

"But how do we get inside?" Quinn asked.

"After the lightning rod is in place, we'll create a distraction, and when the guard comes to see what's the matter, you guys slip through the gate."

Skip thought for a moment and then nodded. "That's okay with me."

Quinn shrugged. "Me, too."

Katie knew this wasn't the moment to mention she was afraid of heights, so she swallowed hard and said, "Count me in."

Thunder rumbled off in the distance and all four of them looked up at the sky. The western horizon was boiling with clouds.

"We better move fast," Trevor murmured. "We don't want to miss the storm."

Skip led the way to the spot just behind the funhouse. He and Trevor quickly snapped the metal sections together. Trevor looped one end of the roll of baling wire through a metal hole at the base of the pole. Then Skip lifted the pole upright. It was at least twenty feet long.

"Perfect," Trevor said. "If this doesn't attract lightning nothing will."

Skip leaned the pole against the side of the fence, then motioned to Katie and Trevor. "Now it's your turn. You'll have to slide onto the funhouse roof from the top of the fence."

Trevor sprang at the fence like a monkey, clinging to the links with his fingers. Then he scurried nimbly up the side until he reached the top. "Give the pole a shove."

Skip gave the base of the pole a mighty heave and it flew up between Trevor's hands. He deftly guided it onto the roof, then gathered up the baling wire, which dangled behind like a relaxed spring. Finally Trevor jumped off the top of the fence onto the roof and disappeared from view.

"Okay, Katie. It's your turn," Skip urged hoarsely. "Go!"

Katie was reaching for the fence when a bolt of lightning lit the sky. She leapt back in fright, then held her breath and counted, "One one-thousand, two one-thousand, three one-thousand, four one-thousand — " A distant rumble answered her.

Quinn tapped her on the shoulder. "Katie, I think I hear footsteps."

"But the lightning," Katie said, not wanting to even touch the metal fence, let alone climb it. "I could get electrocuted."

"It's at least four miles away," Skip replied. "Trust me. You're safe."

"Safe from lightning, maybe," Katie said under her breath. "But not from danger."

"Hurry, Katie," Quinn pleaded, gripping her head with her hands. "He's coming. I can feel it."

That was all she needed to hear. Katie pulled herself up the side of the chain link fence and, swinging one leg across the top, straddled it.

Her leg brushed the roof of the funhouse and she shuddered so violently that the fence wobbled back and forth. Katie was suddenly overcome with a sickening dizziness.

"Oh, you guys, I'm so afraid," she moaned. "Of

heights. Of lightning. Of the funhouse. Of everything." Her voice cracked as she said, "I can't help you. I'm just not strong enough."

"You are, Katie," Quinn called.

"Please," she moaned. "I want to go home."

"Think of something else," Quinn ordered. "Like Lila Wilkins and her prize-winning cat, Purrspicacity."

Lila and Katie had been archenemies since first grade, when snobby Lila made fun of Katie's Easter outfit and Katie pushed her in the mud.

"Lila makes me sick," Katie said in a shaky voice. "And that cat's a joke. His fur fell out last winter and it still hasn't grown back. He looks like a rat."

"That's the spirit," Quinn encouraged. "Now go."

Thinking about Lila let Katie forget about how high up she was. She slowly stuck out one hand and clutched the edge of the funhouse roof. Then with the fence shaking back and forth she pulled herself to a standing position.

"Trevor?" she called into the darkness. "Give me a hand, please."

There was no answer and she called more urgently. "Trevor, please help. I'm losing my balance."

A flash of lightning crackled across the sky above her head and Katie screamed in alarm. Suddenly the fence bent backward, sending her sprawling onto the roof. She hit with a loud thud and for one terrifying moment, Katie thought the roof was going to collapse.

After several terrible seconds, Katie slowly raised her head. A little boy in knickers and a sweater was staring down at her impassively, his hands in his pockets.

"Tommy," she gasped, putting her hand to her chest. "You nearly scared me half to death."

"Tommy-boy scares everyone." He scratched behind one ear. "It makes Tommy-Tom-Tom sad."

"What are you doing on the roof?" Katie asked, peering into the darkness for Trevor. He was no-where to be seen. The lightning rod was right where Skip had tossed it, half on and half off the roof.

"Skip?" she hissed over the side of the roof. No answer came. "Quinn? Skip? Can you hear me?" Katie's chest began to tighten with panic. "Where is everyone?"

Tommy bent toward Katie and whispered, "They can run-run-run. But they can't-can't-can't hide."

His dull eyes filled Katie with fear. "What's that supposed to mean?"

"So you came back," a voice declared from behind her. Katie spun around to see Annie Ent-whistle sitting on a camp stool at the center of the flat roof. She looked as if she'd been waiting for

Katie. "I warned you. But it's hard to resist a carnival, isn't it?"

Katie was still shaken by Tommy's bizarre statement and could only stammer, "Y-y-yes, I guess. Well, no — "

"Tommy!" Annie barked at the little boy. "Get back into the funhouse with ya."

"But Tommy wants to stay with you," he said, slipping his hand into Katie's. "Please, can I?"

"Get away from here," Annie hissed. "I'm taking care of this one. Now get!"

Tommy spat at the old hag's feet, then darted to the far side of the flat roof. Before he shimmied down the drainpipe, he said, "Tommy-Tommy-Tom is mad."

Brilliant yellow veins of lightning arced across the sky. Katie knew that the storm was nearly upon them. But where were Trevor, Skip, and Quinn?

Annie Entwhistle rose from her stool and inched closer to Katie. "You ought to be more careful."

"Wha — what do you mean?" Katie said, stumbling backward. Now she was really frightened. If Trevor was to have created a disturbance, he would have done it by now. And Skip and Quinn should have been nearby.

Annie pointed one long bony finger in the direction Tommy had gone. "That little boy is no ordinary little boy. He's Greywold's servant." She stopped suddenly and cocked her head. "Now Greywold knows you're here."

The image of the magician's cruel face painted on the funhouse sign flashed through Katie's mind, and her blood froze. "Where are my friends?" she demanded. "What have you done with them?"

"Greywold has them," Annie whispered, releasing her hold on Katie. "And now Christina, Ajax, and Reynard will be back with the others."

"Who are they?"

"Greywold's freaks — the bearded fat lady, the strong man, and Reynard, the dog-faced boy."

"You know them?" Katie asked, staring wide-eyed at Annie.

"After Phantasmagoria fell apart, we were the six that remained with Greywold. Me, Tommy, the freaks — and Gogol, the tattooed man."

Thunder boomed straight overhead and Katie leapt three inches off the roof. Annie hardly noticed.

"All six of us trapped for eternity in Greywold's funhouse."

The sky cracked with thunder again. The wind picked up and was blowing so hard, Katie feared she might be blown off the roof. She bent at the waist, trying to resist its force. "But you're not trapped. Why don't you run?"

Annie spoke as if she were in a trance. "Somebody has to be Greywold's eyes and ears. I am his seer."

"Seer," Katie repeated.

Annie nodded slowly. "Where e'er we go, I keep watch. Looking for suitable additions to Greywold's collection."

"Collection?" Katie's voice was barely a whisper. "What does he collect?"

"People."

"Like the ballerina and the Indian in the front hall — "

"Exactly."

Katie could barely catch her breath. "You mean, they were from towns like Wheaton?"

"All of them went to the carnival, bought their tickets, entered the funhouse, and were never heard from again."

Terrible images were swirling in Katie's head. She gasped, "And those people in the little town calling for help in the little houses, and the family in the painting — "

Annie grinned toothlessly. "I found them all." The old woman's eyes, which had been cloudy gray, suddenly blazed red as her hand shot out and clutched Katie's wrist. "And now I've found you."

"But I thought you were on my side," Katie stammered as she tried to free her wrist from the old hag's grasp.

"Ye thought wrong," a voice chuckled behind her.

Katie spun to see the tattooed man standing on the roof, grinning.

Annie gestured to Katie. "Our plan worked. I warned her to stay away and she came back with her friends."

The tattooed man moved toward Katie. "Now we've got all of you."

"Trevor!" Katie screamed, hoping against hope that what they were saying was a lie. "Quinn! Skip!"

"You can shout all you like but your friends won't hear you," Annie hissed. "They're part of the funhouse now. Just like you'll be."

"We'll see about that." Katie lurched sideways. She grasped the lightning rod in one hand and swung it at Annie. The pole was long and unwieldy but it hit its mark.

"Unngh!" Annie Entwhistle staggered sideways, clutching her shoulder. She raised her head and her eyes had turned red once more. "Why you nasty little brat. You'll regret that. Gogol! Get her!"

The tattooed man moved in on Katie.

"Stay away!" she shouted, holding up the lightning rod with both hands.

Gogol quickly grabbed the end of the lightning rod as thunder and lightning erupted overhead.

Katie pulled for all she was worth but the lightning rod came apart and she stumbled backward onto the roof.

Crack!

For a moment Katie thought the explosion was thunder but it was the rickety roof giving way beneath her. Before she could scramble to safety, the ceiling caved in and she plummeted into the gaping darkness below.

Chapter Twelve

"**A**m I dead?"

The painful effort of moving her lips was enough to convince Katie she was alive. The rotten roof panels that had given way beneath her weight had broken her fall and probably saved her life. She lay cradled in the middle of a thick pile of weathered gray shingles.

"Making that lightning rod was the stupidest idea in the world," Katie muttered as she noticed a section of it lying near her. The rest of the makeshift pole stuck out across the gaping hole in the roof. The baling wire dangled uselessly down into the room.

"Why didn't we think it out?" Katie asked herself. "We should have gotten help. We should never have come back to the funhouse."

She raised up on one elbow and tried to focus on the room around her. A bluish haze hung in the room. Katie could barely make out rectangular shapes hovering in the thin mist.

"Oh, no," Katie moaned as she realized she'd fallen into the dreaded Hall of Mirrors. She struggled groggily to her feet. "No . . . I can't be here."

Suddenly the room filled with a thick cold smoke that froze Katie to the marrow. Swirling like a whirlpool, the fog gradually took the shape of a human skull. Two eyes glowed in the head like fiery hot coals.

"Who — who are you?" Katie stammered, pressing herself against the wall.

"Who am I?" the specter hissed in a voice that seemed to reverberate through the walls of the funhouse. "I am the noises rustling under your bed at night. I am the creak in your closet door, the footsteps that follow you home in the dark, the fleeting shadow that you see out of the corner of your eyes. Whenever it's dark and lonely I am with you. I am your midnight fear, I am your worst nightmare. Call me — "

"Greywold," Katie whispered.

The flesh covering the skull began to crawl and squirm like thousands of insects, until finally it formed a face. The inhuman lips curled into a gruesome smile.

Every cell in Katie's body screamed, "Run!" But when she turned to flee, a huge figure stood in her way. It was the strong man.

"Skip!" Katie cried. "You're here — and you're alive!" She threw her arms around the tall strong man. "You don't know how happy I am to see you."

Skip stood motionless, like a mannequin. His frozen expression was just like the faces on the wax figures she'd seen in the entryway that afternoon.

"What's he done to you?" Katie whispered.

"This is not your friend," the voice of Greywold rasped. "This is Ajax. He's part of my collection. I have them back and I'll never let them go."

Katie panicked. If the three freaks had been returned, where were her friends?

"Trapped," Greywold answered as if he'd read her mind. "Imprisoned forever in glass."

"The mirrors!" Katie murmured. "Of course."

"And soon you will join them."

"Never!" Katie dropped to her knees and crawled for a small door at the end of the room. She opened it and disappeared into the darkness inside.

She expected the door to lead her into the miniature village she had visited that afternoon. But instead of seeing tiny cars and trucks scuttling between perfect little white houses, Katie found herself in her own bedroom.

"It can't be." Katie reached for the blue-and-white quilt her grandmother had given her for her tenth birthday. The soft fabric rustled between her fingers. "But it seems so real."

Katie pressed her hand to her forehead. It was

very warm, and moist with sweat. "Maybe I didn't leave my room, and I truly am home sick in bed." She moved to the door, which was shut, and called through it, "Mom? Mom, are you there?"

"I'll be right in honey," she heard her mother's voice answer. "I'm still looking for a thermometer."

But she found the thermometer, Katie thought to herself, reaching for the doorknob. *Or at least I thought she had.*

Katie tugged opened the door to call back to her mother and found herself face-to-face with a rotting corpse dressed in a clown suit. Roaches swarmed out of the eye sockets. Then the whole hideous apparition lurched toward Katie.

Katie screamed and leapt back out of the way. She wasn't in her room.

It was still the funhouse. "Get me out of here!"

The corpse on the floor suddenly turned its head and a voice sounding like a tape player with nearly dead batteries said, "You can't escape the funhouse. You're mine. All mine."

It was Greywold. He had tapped her own memories to re-create her bedroom. Now he was trying to frighten her out of her mind and into his clutches. Katie squeezed her eyes shut and repeated her mother's words. "An illusion. That's all you are. A trick to fool audiences. But I won't be fooled." She stuck out her hands and inched forward trying to find a way out.

Someone clasped her arm firmly. "I'm taking you to Quintero's office. You're in big trouble."

"Fritz?" Katie's eyes popped open. "Fritz Lazarde?"

The stocky hall monitor from school was leading her down the hall toward the principal's office. Lockers lined both walls and the familiar smell of hot rolls from the cafeteria filled the air.

"How did I get here?" she demanded.

"You cut class, remember?" Fritz replied, pulling her relentlessly down the hall. Katie could only see the back of his head in front of her. "You and Quinn."

"But I never skip school. I have a perfect attendance record." Katie yanked her arm away from the boy angrily. "*Wait* a minute."

Fritz spun around and Katie gasped in horror. A scaly lizard's head with yellow eyes glared at her. Suddenly the monster bared its teeth and, instead of a tongue, fanged snakes writhed in his mouth, snapping at her viciously.

Katie nearly fainted. She shut her eyes and tried to calm herself by using the logic her mother always used to calm Katie whenever she had a nightmare.

"You're not real," Katie declared. "You're a bad dream. I'm imagining a lizard because everyone calls Fritz Lazarde Lizard-Lips. Greywold knows that. He's only reading my mind."

Katie opened her eyes once more and the illusion was gone. She kept moving down the corridor, hoping to stumble across the way out.

"Katie! Help!"

The voice was coming from the end of a hallway. Katie recognized it immediately. It was Quinn's. She started to turn, then stopped.

"I'm not going to look," Katie said, pressing her hands over her eyes. "You're just another illusion."

"He's got Skip," Katie heard Quinn say as she came closer. "And I don't know what's happened to Trevor."

"I'm not looking," Katie murmured. "You won't fool me again." She felt someone tug at her sleeve.

"Please look at me, Katie," Quinn pleaded. "Please tell me you're real."

Katie opened one eye slightly and peeked. The fat bearded lady was gone and in her place stood a very disheveled, very upset Quinn.

"Is it really you?" Katie whispered, trying not to hope too desperately.

Quinn put her hands to her face. "Oh, Katie, I don't know anymore," she said shakily. "So much has happened." Two tears trickled down her cheeks, leaving a trail of dark mascara behind.

A violent clap of thunder rocked the entire building and the ceiling above their heads creaked dangerously. Quinn shot a worried glance upward. "Please, let's get out of here. I'm so scared."

Katie cautiously touched her friend's face. "It really *is* you!"

"Yes!" Quinn cried. "My hair's a mess, my clothes look terrible, and I'm scared out of my mind. But it's me."

Katie laughed out loud in spite of herself. Only Quinn would worry about how she looked at a moment like this. Katie gleefully wrapped her arms around her friend's shoulders.

"I can't tell you how glad I am to see you," she cried. "And in your real body, too."

"Come on, let's go." Quinn caught hold of Katie's hand and pulled her back down the hall.

"Where are we going?" Katie asked uncertainly.

"I saw a way out," Quinn replied. "There isn't much time."

Katie stumbled blindly after Quinn. She was so relieved to have finally found her friend that she didn't think to question the route they were taking.

"There's the door!" Quinn cried.

Katie looked up and saw an archway marked by a neon sign that flashed EXIT across the top. "Oh, thank goodness!" Just a few more feet and Katie would be out of the funhouse forever.

Lightning flashed through the open archway and the air was filled with the acrid smell of burning ozone. Katie ignored it and leapt through the opening, crying. "We're free!"

Two tendrils coiled themselves around her

wrists. The hand she'd been holding wasn't Quinn's but only a bloody stump.

"Got you!"

Annie, Gogol, and Tommy stood in front of Katie, grinning triumphantly. Above their heads rain poured through a jagged hole in the ceiling. Each flash of lightning lit up the framed glass lining the walls. She was back in the Hall of Mirrors, right where she'd started.

"No, no, no." Katie wailed, twisting her head back and forth. "It can't be."

The three figures shimmered and shook in the light, then slowly merged into one person. Katie stared openmouthed at a gaunt figure cloaked in black. A brilliant ruby ring shone on his gloved left hand. His face was hidden by the hood of his cloak.

Suddenly Katie realized that *all* of the characters she'd met in the funhouse had been illusions. There was no Annie, no Gogol, no Tommy. Only Greywold.

"You've gone everywhere and nowhere," Greywold said. "You wanted to find your friends . . . so here they are." The magician gestured to three mirrors hanging on the opposite wall. The frames spun like tops and finally came to rest facing Katie.

"Oh, no!" she gasped.

Staring at her from within the glass were the real shapes of Trevor, Quinn, and Skip. Each one had a look of complete terror frozen on their face.

Greywold pointed at the mirrors again. Three blue balls of fire shot out of his fingertips and passed through the air toward the mirrors. As the eerie light flickered and danced around the glass, Katie watched her friends flinch.

"They're mine. All mine." Greywold raised his arm once more and something in Katie snapped. Her fear vanished. All she knew was that her friends were being hurt and she had to stop it.

Katie grabbed the section of flagpole that had fallen with her through the roof. She swung for all she was worth at the figure of Greywold.

"Take that! And that!"

Greywold split in two, and the pole passed through thin air. Katie swung again and again, and each time the magician split into more and more images of himself until finally there were a hundred Greywolds, taunting her with mocking laughter.

"You can't fight me," they chorused. "Give up."

"No. I won't!" Katie screamed, redoubling her efforts.

Outside, the storm reached a crescendo of howling wind and wall-shaking thunder. Water gushed through the opening in the roof and still Katie kept swinging. She flailed blindly, wiping the rain from her eyes between each futile blow.

Suddenly Greywold became one again, and he

wrenched the pole out of her hands. With a triumphant cry, the magician thrust it high into the air, preparing to strike at Katie.

Crack!

A bolt of lightning zigzagged through the hole in the roof, hitting the pole directly. A force, like a blast of dynamite, knocked Katie to the floor.

"Aaaaaaaaaah!"

Greywold was stuck fast to the lightning rod, unable to move. Fiery arcs of electricity radiated from his body and sparks showered the room.

Then mirror after mirror exploded. Glass flew everywhere, and Katie shut her eyes and covered her head to avoid being cut.

"My mirrors! My precious mirrors!"

Greywold's screams were nearly drowned out by the swirling wind that sucked the air out of the building. Katie clung desperately to the floor, certain that she was caught in the grasp of a furious tornado. As she listened, the magician's voice seemed to rise higher and higher in the air above her.

"Finished? It's not possible, it's — "

Suddenly it was over. The sound was gone and the wind was still. Even the rain had stopped.

Katie lay on the weathered floorboards of the old building for several minutes, afraid to open her eyes. Finally she uncovered her head. Greywold was gone. She knew it without even looking.

It felt as if a heavy weight had been lifted off her chest.

"Smoke and mirrors," Katie said softly. "That's all magic is — smoke and mirrors."

In the magician's place stood her three very confused, but very real friends.

Skip, Quinn, and Trevor patted their arms and legs tentatively, as if they weren't sure they were real. Slowly Trevor straightened his glasses and peered at Katie.

"Trevor?" Katie whispered. "Please say it's you."

He shook his head and felt his face with his hands. "I think it's me. It sure feels like me. What happened?"

Tears welled up in Katie's eyes. "It worked," she said, wrapping her arms around her friends. "The lightning rod worked."

Chapter Thirteen

No one believed their story. When they tried to tell their parents about the terrible visions they'd seen that night, the four friends were met with angry responses.

Katie was confined to her room after school for a week. Trevor's mom and dad were furious about the damage Trevor had done to his house and his dad's trench coat, and Skip was in hot water for staying out late without permission. Quinn was the only one who wasn't grounded. It was her idea to sneak out one last time to make their pact.

They met at the remains of their old clubhouse and took a solemn vow never to talk about what had happened in the Phantasmagoria Funhouse. Greywold was gone. They'd destroyed him, hadn't they? The evil presence the magician had brought to Wheaton was no more. It was better to just forget the whole terrible nightmare, and go on.

They would have forgotten about it completely — shoving that awful memory to the back recesses of their mind — if it weren't for what happened a year later.

Katie and her mother had gone to the city to shop for a spring wardrobe. The two of them stopped at Dee's Cafeteria for a quick lunch, and that was where Katie saw the newspaper article.

It was just a tiny column on the back page. She wouldn't have noticed it at all if they hadn't been forced to share a table at the crowded cafeteria with an old man, who puffed a smelly cigar as he studied his paper.

"THREE CHILDREN VANISH FROM FAIR-GROUNDS," the headline read. The article went on to describe how three seventh-graders from Fielders Corners, Nebraska (which wasn't far from Wheaton), had gone to a local carnival after school one day, and never come home. The police found no evidence of foul play and suspected that the children might have run away from home. However, several of their friends reported last seeing the missing children talking with some employees of the carnival — a tattooed man, a fortune teller, and a young boy with odd red eyes.

"Oh, *no*," Katie whispered in horror. She leapt up from the table and ran to the nearest telephone booth. Her hands were shaking so hard she could hardly put her quarter in the slot. She punched in the numbers and waited. The phone rang for a very long time. Finally Quinn answered.

"Hello?"

Katie took a deep breath and spoke two words that sent a cold stab of fear through her friend's heart. "He's back . . ."

About the Author

JAHNNA N. MALCOLM is really the pen name for the husband and wife writing team, Jahnna Beecham and Malcolm Hillgartner.

Together they have written over forty books for kids, including the *Bad News Ballet* series for Scholastic, and the mystery series *Hart and Soul*.

Jahnna and Malcolm currently live with their son, Dash, and daughter, Skye, in an old log cabin on a lake in the northwestern corner of Montana.

GET
Goosebumps
by R.L. Stine
Now!